P9-DTJ-225

This book is a work of fiction. Names, characters, places, and incidents either are products of the author's imagination or are used fictitiously. Any resemblance to actual events or locales or persons, living or dead, is entirely coincidental.

# The Mystery Before Christmas

## A Cat in the Attic Mystery

## By

# Kathi Daley

January - 2020
El Dorado County Library
345 Fair Lane
Placerville, CA 95667

# A Cat in the Attic Mystery

The Curse of Hollister House

The Mystery Before Christmas

The Secret of Logan Pond

# Chapter 1

## Monday

"He moves softly through the night, unseen and unheard, leaving gifts for those in need, while the residents of snowy Foxtail Lake slumber beneath blankets piled high to ward off the chill of a Rocky Mountain winter." I turned and looked at the cat I'd been reading aloud to. "What do you think? Too flowery?"

"Meow."

"Yeah, maybe I should back off the descriptors a bit. It's just that I want to grab my readers right from the beginning. Maybe I should just say something like: 'Secret Santa strikes again,' and then talk about the gifts." I paused to consider this. "Honestly, most of the gifts have been delivered by means other than late-night drop-offs, but the imagery of Santa lurking around in the middle of the night is a lot more appealing than the imagery created by a wheelchair being delivered by UPS." I glanced out the window at the falling snow. The little room at the top of the house felt cozy and warm, and it was this feeling I wanted to bring to my readers. I glanced down at my laptop and began to simultaneously type and speak once again. "Not only has the mysterious gift giver, known only as Secret Santa, been busy doling out random acts of kindness to the town's residents, but he also seems to understand exactly what each gift recipient needs. Billy Prescott received a new wheelchair after his mother backed over his old one; Connie Denton was gifted a down payment on the diner where she'd worked for over twenty years and hoped to buy from her boss when he retired and moved off the mountain; Gilda Frederickson found a gift card for a winter's worth of snow shoveling services in her purse after word got out that she'd broken her hip; and Donnie Dingman walked out onto his drive to find a used four-wheel-drive vehicle so he could get to his doctor's appointments even when it snowed. Some are calling this anonymous gift giver an angel come to earth during this holiest of seasons, while others are certain the late-night Samaritan actually is Santa Clause himself." I looked at the cat. "Better?"

The cat jumped down off the desk where he'd been sitting and watching me work, and headed toward the attic window, which was cheerily draped with white twinkle lights. Apparently, my honorary editor was done listening to my drivel for the day. I supposed I didn't blame him. It did seem like I was trying too hard to find the perfect words to describe the phenomenon that had gripped my small town for the past several weeks.

I got up from the desk and joined the cat on the window seat. It felt magical to sit in the window overlooking the frozen lake as fresh snow covered the winter landscape. Great-aunt Gracie had strung colorful lights on one of the fir trees in the yard, bringing the feel of the season to the frozen landscape. Combined with the white lights draped over every shrub outdoors, and the white lights I'd strung around the window and along the ceiling of the attic, it felt like I was working in a magical fairyland.

"Maybe instead of a whimsical piece filled with artful words, I should do more of a hard-hitting expose," I suggested to the cat. "Everyone knows about the mystery person who has been gifting the citizens of Foxtail Lake with the exact gifts they need the most, but no one knows who he is. Maybe I, Calliope Rose Collins, should work to unmask the Good Samaritan. I know the people he has helped with his good deeds would welcome the chance to thank him. He really is changing lives. He deserves recognition for that."

"Meow." The cat began to purr loudly as he crawled onto my lap. I gently stroked his head as I considered the past two months and the changes I'd seen in my own life.

Two months ago, I'd come back to Foxtail Lake after a terrible accident had shattered my world. At the time, I was a broken woman simply looking for somewhere to lick my wounds, but in the two months I'd been here, not only had I finally begun to accept my new situation, but I'd made quite a few strides in my effort to reinvent my life as well. While my years as a concert pianist would always hold a special place in my heart, I loved volunteering at the Foxtail Lake Animal Shelter, and I adored my new career as a columnist for the local newspaper, a role I'd earned after I'd helped my childhood friend, Cass Wylander, solve not only a present-day murder but the twenty-year-old murder of my best friend, Stella Steinmetz, as well. After the case was solved, I wrote about my experience, the local newspaper picked it up, and as they say, the rest is history. The article was so well received that I'd been offered a weekly column to fill with whatever subject matter I chose.

Unfolding myself from the window, I crossed the room and sat back down at the old desk that I'd shoved into the center of the attic to use as my temporary office. The article on Secret Santa would be the fourth article I'd written for the newspaper. The first article on Stella's murder had been published in mid-November, followed by an article about the missing dogs from the animal shelter where I volunteered, and then an investigative piece relating to the controversy surrounding the misappropriation of the funds which should have been earmarked to pay for the annual tree lighting which was due to run this week. The stories I wrote weren't the hard-hitting exposes a real investigative reporter might pen, but I had helped Cass find Stella's killer, I had found the missing dogs and the man who took them, and I had found the cleverly disguised missing money after it was announced the annual tree lighting would be canceled due to a lack of funds.

Of course, Cass had helped with Stella's murder and the missing dogs. He would probably have been happy to help with the missing funds as well, but that story broke right about the same time Buford Norris turned up dead. Buford was an ornery sort who tended to drink too much, so after his body was found buried beneath the snow, most people just assumed he'd passed out and froze to death. But Cass wasn't quite as sure as some of the other town folk were that Buford had passed out on his own. Investigating the man's death as possible foul play wasn't sitting well with the sheriff or the mayor, but Cass was a conscientious sort who wasn't going to close a case based on a maybe.

"Is Paisley coming for a piano lesson today?" Great-aunt Gracie called up the stairs.

"She is," I called back down the stairs of the large lakefront home I'd grown up in. "Anna has dance after school, so her mother can't give Paisley a ride home. I was planning to pick her up."

"I'm going to run to the market. I can pick her up if you'd like."

"That'd be great."

Paisley Holloway was our ten-year-old neighbor who was living with her grandmother after her mother passed just before Thanksgiving. Gracie and I were doing what we could to help out since the grandmother had her own health issues to deal with. Most days, Paisley got a ride to and from school with her friend, Anna, but on the days Anna's mother was unable to provide a ride, Gracie or I picked her up from school. On the days we picked her up, we usually brought her here to the house, helped her with her homework, and generally did what we could to make things easier for everyone involved. It really was a terrible situation. One that no ten-year-old should have to live through. I'd lost my parents when I was young as well, so I knew better than most how important it was to have a safe harbor in the storm.

"Is Alastair up there with you?" Aunt Gracie called after a few minutes had passed.

I looked at the longhaired black cat who'd jumped back onto the desk next to me. "He is."

"Okay, make sure he doesn't get out. There is a big storm blowing in, and I wouldn't want him to get trapped out in it."

"I'll keep an eye on him," I called. I supposed I should have gotten up and headed downstairs when Gracie first called up since it would have cut down on all the yelling back and forth. "Just send Paisley up when you get back. Alastair and I are working on next week's column."

"Okay. If you see Tom, let him know that dinner will be at six tonight."

Tom Walden was Gracie's groundskeeper, although, in reality, he was so much more. He'd lived on the property with Gracie for more than forty years. Tom and Gracie were friends, good friends who shared their lives. Sometimes I wondered if they weren't something more.

Once Gracie left, I returned my attention to the blank page in front of me. I had to admit the idea of Secret Santa intrigued me. Not only because this particular Santa had already spent tens of thousands of dollars gifting deserving citizens with items they needed but would be unable to buy on their own, but also because he'd been doing it for almost four weeks and so far no one had figured out who he was. There were theories, of course. A lot of them. Based on the monetary value of the gifts, it seemed pretty obvious the Secret Santa was someone of means. Though our town was small, and those who'd lived here for a lifetime tended not to be the sort to acquire a large amount of wealth, the town did tend to attract more than its share of retirees, many of whom were quite wealthy when they arrived. Since I was suddenly determined to identify Secret Santa in my column, I started a list of possible "suspects" after considering the monetary outlay.

The first name to come to mind was Carolyn Worthington. Carolyn was an heiress who'd lived in Boston until two years ago when her only child, a son in his forties, had died in an accident. Shattered to her core, she realized she needed a complete change, so she bought an estate on the east shore of the lake and then quickly made friends by volunteering in the community. Carolyn was quick to share her wealth and had given a lot of money away in the past, which made her both a good and a poor candidate for Secret Santa. If Carolyn was doing the good deeds, then why the sudden secrecy? Still, given her wealth and her altruistic nature, she was on the top of most of the suspect lists in town.

Then there was Haviland Hargrove, a lifelong Foxtail Lake resident whose grandfather had struck it rich during the gold rush of the nineteenth century. Haviland wasn't as naturally altruistic as Carolyn, but he certainly had the means to buy everything that had been purchased and then some. He was a man in his early eighties, so perhaps he'd decided to spread his wealth around a bit before he passed on.

Dean and Martin Simpson were brothers who'd made a fortune in the software industry. The men lived together in a mansion set in the center of a gated estate. Neither had ever married nor had children and while they didn't go out and socialize a lot, they were pleasant enough and had several good friends in the community, including my friend, Cass, who played poker with them twice a month. Cass didn't think that Dean and Martin were our Secret Santas, but I wasn't so sure about that.

There were a handful of other locals with the means to do what was being done. I supposed that once I developed my list, I'd just start interviewing folks. Someone must know something that would point me in the right direction. I supposed there would be those who would think I should leave well enough alone, and perhaps they would be right, but after stumbling across a really juicy mystery like this one, anyone who knew me knew I was prone to follow the clues to the end.

"Anyone home?" Tom called.

I got up and walked to the top of the stairs. "I'm here. Aunt Gracie went to the market. She said to tell you that dinner will be at six."

"That should work. Did she happen to say what she wanted me to do with the tree ornaments she had me pick up while I was in Lakewood?"

I decided to head down the stairs rather than continuing this conversation as a yelling match. "She didn't say. I'm surprised she wanted additional ornaments. We have boxes of them in the attic."

"I guess these are special. Custom made. I'll just leave them on the dining table for now."

I glanced out the open door at the darkening sky, mindful of Gracie's warning about not letting Alastair out. "I'm sure that is fine. Let me lock the cat in the den, and I'll help you carry everything in."

"I'd appreciate that. It seems your aunt has gone decorating crazy this year."

I looked around the house, which was already decked out with garland, candles, wreaths, and bright red bows. She really had outdone herself. When I'd asked her about it, she'd mumbled something about wanting the place to be cheerful for Paisley, but truth be told, I think she was just happy to have others in the house to celebrate with this year.

"As far as you know, are we still getting the tree this week?" I asked Tom after we headed out into the frigid afternoon.

"As far as I know. If this storm dumps as much snow as it is calling for, then I'm afraid her plan to go into the forest to cut a tree might have to be altered. Walter has some nice ones in his lot. I took a look while I was there to pick up the branches Gracie wanted for the mantle."

"I would think a tree from Walter's lot would be just fine. If we can cut one, we will, but if not, we'll work together to sell Gracie on the tree lot idea." I picked up the first of five boxes in the back of Tom's truck. "I'm really happy she is enjoying the holiday so much this year, but I'm afraid she is going to overdo. Not only has she gone crazy decorating, but she signed up to be the co-chair for the Christmas in the Mountains event as well."

"Your aunt has a lot of energy. I'm sure she'll be fine. We just need to be sure to help out as much as we can."

"I guess."

"Gracie wants you to have the perfect Christmas. Like the ones the two of you shared when you were younger. This is important to her."

I glanced up at the sky filled with snow flurries as I started toward the house. "It's important to me as well, and I do plan to help out as much as I can. Of course, researching Secret Santa is going to keep me busy. I think I've pretty much decided to focus on figuring out who Secret Santa is rather than the gifts he has delivered. You haven't heard anything have you?"

Tom set his box on the table next to mine, and we both turned around to go for the next load.

"Everyone seems to have an opinion, but I haven't heard that anyone has come up with any proof as to the identity of Secret Santa if that is what you are asking. The guys down at the lodge think it might be Fisher."

I raised a brow. "Ford Fisher? Why do the guys think it's him? As far as I know, the man isn't rich." Ford Fisher used to own one of the pubs in town before it sold, so I imagined he'd done okay in terms of saving for retirement, but I doubted he had tens of thousands of dollars to give away.

"I think Ford might have more stashed away than one might think. There is a lot of money in alcohol, and Ford has lived simply for much of his life. In my mind, he doesn't have the right temperament to be Secret Santa, but he has been acting oddly lately, which is why I think the guys at the lodge suspect him."

We headed back to the house with the second load of boxes. "Acting oddly, how?" I wondered.

"Secretive. Evasive. He hasn't shown up at the lodge in weeks, and when some of the guys went by his place to see if he was okay, he told them he was fine but didn't even invite them in. I've called him several times, even left messages, but he hasn't called me back."

"Sounds like he might be depressed. Do you know if he suffers from depression?" I set my box next to the others on the table.

"Not that I know of. Ford's always been a real social sort. Other than those few times when he was too hungover to make it to the lodge, he's pretty much been there every Wednesday and Friday since I've been going. Not that I go every week. Sometimes Gracie and I do something, but Ford is a real regular."

"It sounds like you and your friends might be right to be worried about him. I'd continue to check on him if he doesn't start coming around. Having said that, in my mind, his overall mood doesn't seem to have a Secret Santa feel."

Tom headed back out for the final box. I tagged along after him in spite of the fact there was just one box left to fetch.

"Yeah," Tom agreed. "The idea of him being Secret Santa doesn't sit quite right with me either. I hope he isn't ill. He didn't say he was feeling poorly, but that could explain his absences."

"Wasn't Ford friends with Buford?" I asked. "Maybe he is just missing the guy."

"Maybe," Tom agreed. "Ford and Buford went at it like two old junkyard dogs most of the time, but in the end, I guess you could say they were friends. Best friends even. I don't suppose Cass has proven one way or another what happened to Buford."

I shook my head. "On the one hand, Buford had been drinking on the night he died and could very well have wandered out into the blizzard, passed out, and froze to death. On the other hand, Buford had a bump on his head that looked as if it had been inflicted by someone hitting him with a heavy object."

"Could he have hit his head when he passed out?" Tom asked.

"He could have, but the position his body was found in and the location of the bump doesn't tend to support that theory. Of course, Buford could have bumped his head earlier in the day, and the fact that he had a knot the size of a jawbreaker doesn't necessarily mean that injury was enough to cause him to fall to the ground in a state of unconsciousness. At this point, Cass is following the idea that Buford was hit on the head, blacked out, and then froze to death. I guess we'll just have to wait to see where his investigation ends up. I'm sure if Buford simply passed out on account of all the alcohol he drank, that scenario will float to the surface at some point." I looked up as the sound of a car approaching permeated the still air. "That must be Gracie. Paisley will be with her. Maybe we can talk about this some more over dinner."

"That'd be fine. The truth as to what happened to Buford has been weighing on my mind. It'd be nice to know one way or the other."

"Yes," I agreed. It would be nice to know for certain what had caused a man who'd lived here for most of his life to simply perish in an early but not all that spectacular storm. I knew the mayor was pushing the idea that Buford's death was nothing more than a terrible accident. I supposed I didn't blame him. The town was just beginning to recover from the murder of twelve-year-old Tracy Porter. If it was determined that Buford had been murdered as well, it would most definitely bring back the fear and paranoia that had permeated the town after Tracy's death. Cass wasn't the sort to simply grasp onto the easy answer; he was the sort to want nothing short of the truth. Sometimes I wondered if his dogged commitment to following his instincts rather than the dictate of his boss was going to get him fired. I supposed that it was more important to Cass to be true to his convictions than it was to keep the job he seemed to do better than anyone else did. I supposed I really admired him for that. In fact, the more I got to know Deputy Cass Wylander, the more convinced I was that my childhood friend had grown into a man I could not only respect but grow to love if I was interested in that sort of thing, which I wasn't.

# Chapter 2

## Tuesday

The Foxtail News was a small regional newspaper with only four employees in addition to the owner if you counted me, and given the fact that I only wrote one column a week at this point, I supposed it was generous to count me in the mix. A man named Garrett Heatherton, who'd partially retired and left the management of the business to his son, Dex, owned the newspaper. Garrett had run the place much the same for the thirty-some-odd years he'd been actively working in the business, but now that Dex had taken over the day-to-day operations, he was determined to put the Foxtail News on the map. A lofty goal I will admit given the limited circulation of the tiny rural area served by the newspaper, but a goal he worked hard for every day.

In addition to Dex, there was a full-time reporter named Brock Green. Garrett had hired Brock when Dex was still in college and felt more than just a bit slighted that he hadn't been chosen to take over as managing editor when Garrett decided to take a step back. I could sense the tension between Dex and Brock at times, but the tension seemed to be rooted in competition, which made both men work harder, so I supposed it worked out okay in the end.

In addition to Garrett, who still oversaw things; Dex, who ran the ship; and Brock, who handled the heavy lifting; there was a woman named Gabby King, who answered the phone and handled the clerical stuff.

"Morning, Gabby," I greeted the woman with short blond curls that framed her face.

"Morning, Callie." Gabby hung a bright red bulb on the fir she'd been decorating. "Dex has been looking for you."

I paused to take in the scent of fir mingled with the familiar scents of stale coffee, which was always present; tobacco, from Brock's cigars; and ink, in spite of the fact that the old offset press hadn't been used in years. "The place looks really nice. I love the big red bows."

"I figured I spend more of my day here than I do at home, so I might as well create the Christmas spirit here too. I started with a wreath for the door, but it looked lonely, so I brought in the garland and bows. Once I got that far, the rest seemed inevitable."

"Well, I think it looks fantastic."

"Dex was hesitant at first. You know how he is about professionalism, but I think he is warming up to the idea now that I have things arranged."

"I'm sure Dex will enjoy the decorations once he relaxes a bit. It has been a tense year for him taking over as managing editor. I think there is a lot of pressure on him to do well."

"I know you're right."

"I suppose I should go and see what he wants. Is he in his office?" I asked.

"He is." Gabby glanced at the paper bag I still held in my hands. "I don't suppose those are Aunt Gracie's muffins?"

"They are." I set the bag on Gabby's desk. "There are plenty to share." I turned and headed down the hallway. It was a long, dark, narrow passage that led to an employee breakroom and several offices. There was the old pressroom at the end of the hallway, where the offset press that had been used for years to print the newspaper still sat.

"Good, I'm glad you're here," Dex greeted as soon as I poked my head in the doorway to his office. "How is the Secret Santa feature going?"

"It's going," I hedged. I'd been playing with different ideas and concepts for days but still hadn't settled on anything that really clicked. "I've been spending some time really trying to nail down the angle I should take," I elaborated. "Initially, I was going to write about the members of the community who've received gifts, but now I'm thinking about writing about Secret Santa himself. Who is this guy? Why is he spending what has already amounted to a small fortune gifting members of our small town with the items they seem to need the most?"

Dex grinned, his dark brown eyes sparkling in delight. "I'm happy to hear you've been thinking along those lines because that is exactly what I was going to speak to you about. I received a call from my buddy at The Denver Post. He's heard the stories relating to our Secret Santa and is interested in piggybacking on our feature. In fact, he wants us to expand on it and do a series of articles."

"A series?"

"Three in all." He ran a hand through his thick brown hair. "And, the best part is that he wants to run the series in the Post. This could be huge for us. Really huge."

"Wow, that is big," I admitted, settling a hip on the edge of the desk. "Did he say what he had in mind?" My mind was already racing with ideas to expand my story and create a series of articles, but I was still interested in what Dex had to say.

"As I mentioned, he wants three articles, the first of which will be due on Monday of next week. He suggested that the article next week focus on the recipients of the gifts. He wants a real in-depth look. Who are these people? Why might Secret Santa have chosen them to be recipients of his altruism? How will the gift they received enhance or change their lives?"

"Sounds doable." I moved over to the chair across from the desk and sat down. My heart was racing and palms sweating, but I honestly didn't know if I was excited or terrified. A series in the Post! This really was a huge opportunity.

"His idea for the first article seems pretty straight forward, so I am inclined to head in that direction. And then the following Monday, he wants to build momentum with an article relating to the hunt for Secret Santa. Really bring the mystery aspect into play by featuring interviews of those members of the community suspected of being Secret Santa. Who are these people? Why do the locals suspect them of being Secret Santa? What do they have to say about the rumors, and what sort of conclusions has the reporter come to based on those interviews?"

"Again, that seems manageable. I've already started a list. And for the final article?"

"The column due on December 23$^{rd}$ will be published in both the Foxtail News and the Post on December 24$^{th}$. Basically, he is looking for the big reveal as to who Secret Santa actually is and why he or she has been gifting such high dollar items to the residents of Foxtail Lake."

I sat back in my chair and really let this whole thing sink in. If I was totally honest, I'd begun to feel just a tiny bit of panic.

"I wanted to talk to you about the series first since it was your idea," Dex continued, "but now that the Post is interested in reprinting the articles, the Secret Santa storyline has become a pretty big deal. I know you are new to journalism, and I am concerned that this might be too much for you. It's not too late to turn this series over to Brock. He does have a lot more experience than you do, so I suspect he might be able to deal with the pressure of a tell-all feature better."

I narrowed my gaze while nibbling gently on my bottom lip, a nervous habit I reverted to frequently.

"So, what do you think?" Dex asked.

What did I think? On the one hand, writing a series of articles that would be reprinted in the Post seemed intimidating. I'd only been a journalist for four weeks, and it wasn't like I had any formal education to fall back on. On the other hand, I'd been hoping to find a way to work my way into more of a regular position with the paper, and this sounded like a fantastic opportunity. Of course, it was an opportunity predicated on my ability to figure out who Secret Santa really was and then get them to agree to an interview. In my mind, neither of these situations was a given.

"I'd like to run with it," I finally said. "I know that I don't have the experience Brock has, but the articles I've written in the past few weeks have been well received, and you liked the one I turned in yesterday about the missing money for the tree lighting. If I hadn't tracked down the money, the town wouldn't even be having a tree lighting this year. I really think I should be the one to do the Secret Santa series."

Dex hesitated. I could see he might need additional convincing.

"Brock is a fine reporter, and I agree that he has a ton more experience than I do, but he is sort of analytical in his approach to his subject matter. Secret Santa is a human-interest story, and you need someone to get to the heart of the matter and bring the emotion behind the action into play. You need someone like me."

He exhaled loudly. "Okay. I'll let you run with the first story relating to the gift recipients, and then I'll decide what to do after I see how things are progressing. But keep in mind that I basically promised my buddy from the Post that we would have no problem unmasking Secret Santa, which means we have less than three weeks to figure out who Secret Santa is."

"I know."

"It might not be easy to find the proof you'll need to definitively identify the guy."

"I know."

"And if you do manage to finger the guy, you'll still need to get him to agree to an interview. This is a real investigative piece. It is going to take all the sleuthing skills you can muster."

"I know it won't be easy, but I really think I can do this. I want to try. Give me this week and let me write the first article, and then we can talk about how to handle the second and third article at that point."

Dex paused and let out a long, slow breath.

"I'll keep you updated every step of the way," I promised.

"Okay," he said, although he still looked doubtful. "But don't let me down. I have a lot riding on this."

"I know, and I won't." Even as I said the words, I found myself hoping that I could do what I'd just promised I could do and find the man or woman who, to this point, hadn't seemed to want to be found.

# Chapter 3

"So did Gracie get her tree?" Cass asked me later that afternoon while we worked our volunteer shift at the Foxtail Lake Animal Shelter.

"She did. Tom and I ganged up on her yesterday afternoon and talked her into just getting a tree from the lot. It's fresh and well-shaped. I think it will be just fine for the living room, and Paisley and I selected one for the attic as well."

"Have you decorated them yet?" He tossed a ball to a group of labs, who all took off after it.

"Not yet," I smiled as the dogs playfully piled onto each other while trying to be the one to bring the ball Cass had tossed back to him. "Paisley and I are going to decorate the tree in the attic this week, but Gracie wants to wait and decorate the downstairs tree on Saturday. She really wants all of us to do it together, but I had my volunteer shifts today and Friday, and Tom has some sort of event going on over at the lodge tomorrow and Thursday, so we put the tree in the stand and filled it with water, but it is still totally bare. If you don't mind getting bossed around by Gracie for a few hours, we could probably use some help on Saturday if you're free. Gracie insisted on getting the tallest tree in the lot. Of course, I have no idea how we are going to decorate those top branches."

He accepted the ball from a black lab and then tossed it again. "I'd love to come by and help. I am planning to work for a while on Saturday in the hope of getting caught up on my paperwork, but I can probably be done by one or two unless there is a break in Buford's murder case."

A sheltie had wandered over, and I bent over to scratch him behind the ears. "So, are you formally calling Buford's death a murder?"

"Only between you and me. I don't have enough evidence one way or the other to state as much conclusively, and the mayor doesn't want me using the 'M' word unless I absolutely have to."

Kneeling down on the tile floor, I picked up a small terrier that had wandered over for some attention and cuddled him to my chest. "But you think there is something to find?"

Cass nodded. "My gut tells me, yes. I spoke to the coroner. He said that it is likely that the blow to the head that Buford seems to have suffered before his death could have been enough to cause him to pass out. He didn't think it was hard enough to kill him, and he has listed the official cause of death as hypothermia. We did discuss a scenario where Buford was rendered unconscious due to the blow and then froze to death, and the coroner thinks that scenario is very possible. Buford did have alcohol in his system as well, but in the coroner's opinion, he hadn't ingested enough to render him unconscious, although I suppose one could argue that it was the alcohol that impaired his judgment and caused him to be out in the storm in the first place. The mayor is really invested in the idea that the man simply wandered out into the storm while intoxicated, passed out, and froze to death, but I'm less certain of that."

"So if someone did hit Buford, and if that blow to the head is what led to his death, any idea who might be responsible?"

Cass shook his head slowly. "No idea at all. I've been talking to folks who knew Buford, hoping that a motive will appear, but so far all I really know for certain is that a whole lot of people had a beef with the guy, but no one was mad enough to kill him."

"Tom mentioned Ford Fisher. He said he has been acting oddly. Secretive. Evasive. He's been staying home and not interacting with anyone."

Cass narrowed his gaze. "A couple of the guys from over at the bar said something similar. I really can't see Ford killing Buford, but I suppose I ought to stop by and check on him. He is getting on in years, and I worry about his health."

I smiled. "Seems like you worry about everyone in this town for one reason or another."

Cass shrugged. "It's my job to serve and protect. Part of that service includes a healthy dose of worry. Speaking of which, I know that Paisley has been worrying about her grandmother since her mother died. Pamela Keller mentioned it when I stopped by the school to give my talk on winter safety."

Pamela Keller was Paisley's teacher.

"Paisley is understandably having a difficult time. She is sad that her mother didn't get the miracle they hoped for and worried that her grandmother might be next. Gracie and I have been doing what we can to help out with rides and meals and whatnot. I'm not sure what will happen in the long run. Paisley's grandmother is getting on in years, and unlike Gracie, who is as healthy as a horse, Ethel has been dealing with a few health issues of her own."

Cass tossed several balls in quick succession, and the entire group of dogs went after them once again.

"I feel for both Paisley and her grandmother. If there is anything I can do, just let me know. Is someone taking care of her shoveling and plowing?"

I nodded. "A group from the church has been coming by and keeping the walks and drive clear. I think the community as a whole is doing what they can. Hopefully, it will be enough. According to Gracie, Paisley has an aunt who lives in New Jersey who is willing to take her if Ethel decides she can't manage a ten-year-old on her own, but Gracie also said that Paisley doesn't know this aunt and really wants to stay here in a familiar environment where she has friends she can lean on for support."

"I suppose that if Paisley does have to move, she'll make new friends."

I bowed my head. "I guess, but the death of her mother has been hard enough to deal with. She needs time to grieve and to heal. She needs to be in a familiar environment where she feels safe. At least for now."

"I agree." Cass gathered up the balls that had been dropped at his feet and tossed them again. "And hopefully with everyone's help, Ethel will feel she is able to manage." Cass looked at his watch. "I guess we should begin to wrap this up. I promised Naomi I'd take care of the nighttime routine since Hancock is back in town, and the two had made plans."

Naomi Potter owned the shelter, and Hancock was Naomi's sort-of boyfriend. Actually, when Naomi had mentioned him to me, she'd referred to him as her lover.

"So, what is this guy's deal anyway?" I asked. "I know Naomi said he is in Naval Intelligence, but he seems to pop in and out without notice, and he never really says where he's been or how long he might stay."

Cass shrugged. "I don't know any more than anyone else does. The guy just showed up in town one day, met Naomi, and they hit it off, so in spite of the fact he comes and goes like a thief in the night, they've settled into a relationship of sorts. He obviously is not at liberty to say where he has been or where he might be headed next, so those of us who know him, simply don't ask."

I supposed that if Naomi was okay with the arrangement, I was as well, but the whole thing still seemed really odd to me. "I'll take care of the dogs and cats, and you can take care of the rest of the crew," I suggested, remembering the hard time Naomi's llama, Harry, gave me the last time we helped out.

"Sounds like a plan," Cass agreed. "I'll start with the horses." In addition to the dogs, cats, puppies, and kittens always in residence, Naomi currently had a pen full of mules, a couple of cows, two horses, and Harry, who, as I understood it, was here to stay. "Two of the dogs need medication, so I'll take care of that as well," he offered.

"Yeah, that might be best," I agreed.

Cass and I had helped out with the feeding and tucking in of the animals on several occasions, so I was familiar with the routine, but I wasn't all that skilled at administering medication. Other than the meds, and the ornery llama, it was pretty easy since Naomi always left instructions for each animal in terms of the type and amount of food to be presented at each meal pinned to the board in her office. We just needed to distribute the food, check everyone's water supply, clean up any messes we came across, and make sure everyone was tucked in and locked up for the night.

Once that was done, Cass and I usually grabbed a pizza or burger together. Tonight, we opted for pizza. Cass's dog, Milo, was with us as he was most days, but since he was an official police dog, he was allowed to lay quietly under the table while we ate. The restaurant Cass chose was one of my favorites. It had a genuine Italian feel to it, and if you weren't in the mood for pizza, they served pasta dishes as well. Like most of the other businesses in Foxtail Lake, Luigi's was all decked out for the holiday.

"Did you hear that Secret Santa struck again?" the waitress, whose nametag read Giovanna, asked Cass when she came over to take our order.

"I hadn't heard. Who was the lucky recipient this time?" Cass asked.

"Grover Wood. You know how he lost his contracting business a while back when he couldn't continue to do heavy labor after his snowmobile accident."

"Yeah," he replied. "I had heard that. I hope he had savings to see him through."

"He had some, but not enough," Giovanna answered. "In fact, from what I've heard, he was on the verge of losing his house and had even been looking for a place to move to when he found out that Secret Santa had made all his back payments and even paid his mortgage three months ahead."

I realized this meant that someone at the bank probably knew who Secret Santa was. The odds were that Secret Santa had written a check, which could have been mailed in, or he'd made the payments in person. Perhaps a chat with our friendly bank manager was in order.

"Grover is about as happy as I've ever seen anyone," Giovanna continued. "I don't know who is doing these good deeds, but I sure am thankful. Grover is a good guy. He didn't deserve to lose his home."

"It does seem as if Secret Santa knows just what to give those most in need," Cass agreed.

"He's been a godsend, that's for sure. Everyone is talking about the gifts and the people they've helped. Some are referring to the Secret Santa phenomenon as The Foxtail Lake Miracle."

"I guess Foxtail Lake was due for some good karma," I said. "I know Tracy's death was hard on everyone."

"It really was," Giovanna agreed.

"Any idea who Secret Santa might be?" I figured I had to ask.

She vigorously shook her head. "No idea." She looked directly at me. "And even if I did know, I'd never tell."

I had a feeling that protecting the identity of Secret Santa had become a popular trend.

"Seems like your crusade to identify Secret Santa isn't going to make you any friends," Cass pointed out after Giovanna took our order and left.

"I was just thinking the same thing." I'd chatted with him about the series of articles Dex wanted to do leading up to the big reveal and how this could be good for both the newspaper and for me while we'd been playing with the dogs. "I really want to be the one to do the series. Dex is going to do it with or without me, so my refusal to reveal Secret Santa isn't going to keep his identity a secret. And the story idea was mine in the first place. I should be the one to see it through. But I do realize that by outing Secret Santa, I could be damaging my popularity in the community, which is also important to me."

"It does seem as if you are in a tough spot. Any idea what you are going to do?"

I groaned as I leaned back in the booth. "Not really. I suppose I'll just do the first article, which is about the gift recipients, while I continue to look for the man, or woman as it may be, behind the whole thing. And then, once I figure out who Secret Santa really is, I'll decide what to do. Maybe Secret Santa wants to be found. Maybe Secret Santa is actually after the publicity and will be happy to do the interview."

"Then why all the secrecy?" Cass asked.

"I suppose it could be possible that Secret Santa just wants to build hype." Even as I said this, I knew that it most likely wasn't the case, but it certainly would make things easier for me if Secret Santa did want me to out him at some point before my deadline rolled around. "I don't suppose you've heard anything?"

Cass paused, looking me in the eye. "I do hear things from time to time, but I'm not sure I want Secret Santa to be unmasked any more than the rest of the town does."

I slowly exhaled. "I get it. I do. But I could use some help. Dex really wants this series for the Post. It's a big deal for him. It's a big deal for the newspaper. It's even a big deal for me."

Cass laid his hand over mine. "I know. And it is pretty awesome that the Post is interested in running the articles. I'm sure Dex is over the moon at the opportunity to put the Foxtail News on the map."

"So you'll help me?"

He nodded. "Yes. I'll help you, but keep in mind that finding out what really happened to Buford has to be my priority."

"I know, and I respect that. If you need to toss around ideas relating to Buford's death, I'm more than happy to help you with that as well. It seems to me that the real challenge here is going to be to investigate the case while keeping Mayor White off your back."

I didn't know Mayor White well. He hadn't been mayor when I'd lived in Foxtail Lake before, but in the two months since I'd been back, I'd definitely decided that the guy was not someone I respected. It seemed to me that he cared a lot more about keeping up appearances than he did about getting to the truth. I understood that Foxtail Lake was popular with the tourists from the valley due to its small-town appeal and that a murder in the idyllic small town put a damper on the image he was trying to project, but to manipulate the facts relating to a murder just to keep up appearances was downright unethical in my book.

"He has been pretty vocal about the fact that he doesn't want to stir things up now that everything is starting to settle down following Tracy's murder," Cass agreed.

"Personally, I wish the guy would realize that finding justice for Buford if he was murdered is more important than keeping up the illusion that our little town is above such ugliness, but I guess in his mind, keeping his citizens happy is what is going to get him reelected."

"And I suppose to a point, he is not wrong in that assumption." Cass took a sip of his beer. "Let's not ruin our meal with talk about politics. How is Gracie doing with her co-chair responsibilities?"

"Okay," I answered. "The committee that Gracie is co-chairing with Hope Mansfield is handling all the holiday events for the town. The tree lighting is Friday, followed by the opening of the little Santa's Village on Saturday. The Santa's Village will run all month, and the big Christmas in the Mountains event will take place on Main Street the following weekend. It's sort of a big deal, but I guess you know all this since they have done it for years, and you have lived here forever."

"It is a big deal and a lot of work."

"It is. I sense that Gracie is excited about the holiday this year and happy to be involved, but I also get the feeling that now that it is here, she is beginning to feel the pressure of being one of the chairpersons. I plan to help her as much as I can. I think she has the events for this weekend covered, but I suspect she'll need help with the event on Main Street two weekends from now."

"Gracie is one of the most organized and energetic seniors I've ever met. I'm sure she'll do fine, and Hope tends to help chair most of the events in town, so she knows exactly what to do. Since the tree lighting is this Friday, are you still planning on volunteering at the shelter?"

I nodded. "Actually, I am. The tree lighting is at six, so I'm going to go straight over there from the shelter. Maybe we can go together and then grab dinner after."

"I'd like that. Assuming things go smoothly at the tree lighting and I don't have any arrests to process."

I raised a brow. "Do you generally have arrests to process after the tree lighting?"

"Not normally, but there was one year when some college kids from out of town decided to show up blaring their own music. This angered those who were trying to enjoy a holiday moment, causing a rumble of sorts between the locals and the valley kids. And then there was another year when two of the guys from the lodge got into a fistfight over the correct words to one of the carols sung by the group."

"You're kidding," I chucked.

"Dead serious. Folks around these parts take their carols seriously even if they don't always know the words as well as they think they do. Most folks won't haul off and punch the person next to them if they mess up the words, but it has happened."

"Okay. I'll try to be sure I sing the appropriate words if I am going to join in. If I don't know the words, I'll keep quiet. The last thing I want is to spend the weekend in jail for brawling in the street."

# Chapter 4

## Thursday

The snow had begun to fall with impressive intensity by the time Thursday rolled around. It would actually be a perfect day to snuggle up by the fire with Alastair and read, but I had a story to write and a deadline to meet. I'd worked on outlining the first article, which was due on Monday, yesterday, and my plan for today was to interview as many of the gift recipients as I could. I'd called and made appointments with Billy Prescott, Connie Denton, and Gilda Frederickson, and was waiting to hear back from Donnie Dingman and Grover Wood.

"Something smells good," I said to Gracie after coming down to the kitchen.

"I'm baking muffins. The tree lighting is tomorrow, and the Santa's Village opens on Saturday, not to mention that Christmas in the Mountains is in less than two weeks, so the planning committee is meeting to go over everything. I offered to bring muffins. The meeting is at the inn, so Ida and Maude are supplying the coffee."

Ida and Maude Cunningham owned the local inn. I suspected that Christmas in the Mountains was a real moneymaker for them since the inn usually filled up on the weekend of the event.

"I'm really looking forward to all the community events this year," I commented. "I know I said I'd help out, and I know I haven't gotten around to volunteering for anything specifically, so just put me where you need me. I'm planning to make myself available to you for the entire weekend of Christmas in the Mountains."

"Thank you, dear. That is very generous. It might be a good idea to try to attend the volunteer meeting Hope and I are planning for Saturday morning. I suspect that everyone will choose their volunteer duties then."

"Okay. I'll be there. Just tell me when and where."

"The library at ten a.m."

I supposed that made sense since Hope ran the library and would probably need to be nearby in the event one of her volunteers had a problem. "Are we still going to decorate the big tree in the living room after that?"

"We are. I'm really looking forward to it."

I smiled. "Me too. I haven't had a Christmas tree since I moved away from Foxtail Lake, and now this year, I have two trees to decorate."

"So, what are your plans for today?" Aunt Gracie asked.

I poured myself a second cup of coffee and then sat down at the kitchen table. "I have a series of interviews set up with Secret Santa recipients. I'm doing my column on how these gifts have affected the lives of those on the receiving end. I'm going to pick Paisley up from school after that. We have a piano lesson today, and then I thought I'd help her with her homework."

"I'm making a big pot of soup for dinner if she wants to stay," Gracie offered.

"That sounds perfect. I'll ask her. I know how much Paisley appreciates the fact that we've integrated her into our family. I think she is happy here. I know she loves her grandmother, but I think there are times that Paisley feels like she's a burden."

"I doubt Ethel feels that way."

"Maybe not, but Paisley is a smart girl. I'm sure she understands that having a ten-year-old underfoot is not always easy. Of course, Paisley is the most mature ten-year-old I've ever met. I actually think she helps Ethel more than she realizes." I glanced out the window at the steadily falling snow. "I guess I should head up and take a shower. My first interview is less than two hours from now."

"Who are you speaking to first?" Gracie asked.

"Gilda Frederickson. She was given an entire season of snow removal. I'm not sure that I've met her before."

"She moved to the area a few years after you moved away. She originally came to Foxtail Lake to help her mother after she had a hip replacement. Gilda's mother passed away maybe five years ago and left her house to Gilda."

I pulled up the address in my mind and tried to recall who used to live there. "Are you talking about Mrs. Ewing?"

"Yes. So you do remember her. Gilda is Mrs. Ewing's daughter. She's a very nice woman. She does a lot of volunteer work in the community. I guess she fell and broke her hip a while back. She is doing better but still has a long recovery ahead of her, which is where the help with the snow removal comes in."

"So, Gilda must be around seventy?"

Gracie nodded. "Yes. I'd say around that. Maybe a few years younger. She worked as a librarian before she moved to Foxtail Lake. After her mother recovered from her surgery, she worked part-time with Hope until she decided to retire and focus on volunteer work. I think you'll enjoy speaking to her. She is well-read and seems to know something about a lot of different topics."

"I'm sure I'll enjoy getting to know her."

"Maybe you should take her some muffins," Gracie suggested. "I have plenty, and I think she might enjoy them."

"I will. Thank you. Muffins will serve as a great ice breaker."

"Be sure to dress warmly," Gracie cautioned. "The high temperature is going to be in the single digits today. In fact, I think the high is supposed to remain in the single digits for the entire weekend, but

I understand there will be a slight warming trend next week.

Well, that was something, at least. I had to admit the bracing cold of a Rocky Mountain winter was going to take some getting used to, but I was still happy to be back in this little town that was feeling more and more like home. During my years in New York, I'd been happy. I'd been chasing a dream that seemed to be within my reach and rarely thought about the mountain home that I'd left behind or the people who lived there. But since my return, I'd found myself wondering why I'd ever wanted to leave in the first place. There are places in the world that I'd enjoyed, but Foxtail Lake was the only place that had ever felt like home.

When I arrived in my bedroom, I found Alastair sleeping on the bed. I felt a little bad that he'd started sleeping with me after I'd arrived back home. He was, after all, Gracie's cat, and I was sure she enjoyed his company. I'd asked her about it early on, and she'd said she was fine with him sleeping with me, but now that I was staying, I sort of felt like I should give him back. Of course, I hadn't done anything to lure the cat to my room, and Gracie hadn't said another word about it, so perhaps I'd just leave well enough alone.

"Cords or jeans?" I asked the cat, holding up two pairs of pants. The cords were old, and I was pretty sure they were out of style by this point, they were dark brown, and lined with fleece, which made them extra warm. I supposed they'd look cute tucked into boots with a wool sweater to top them off.

Alastair yawned but didn't reply or get up, so I settled on the cords, found a sweater to match, gathered my underthings, and headed into the bathroom to shower. By the time I got out of the shower, dressed, and dried my hair, Alastair had joined Gracie downstairs. I was about to head back down myself when I noticed a book lying on my bed. It was a book from my childhood that I was pretty sure had been packed away years ago.

I picked the book up and opened it to a colorful page near the middle. The story was about a young girl who lived in a town that had suffered a great loss and had fallen into darkness. The girl's mother had taken the loss of the town's light hard and had fallen into a state of deep depression. The girl wanted to cheer her mother up and bring the smile back to her face, so she devised a plan to give her a very special gift. The problem was, she didn't have money to buy a gift, so she set out to earn some by doing small chores for her neighbors.

It seemed like a good idea when she'd thought of it, but when she approached her neighbors, who also lived in the town which had been thrust into darkness, she found that, while each neighbor needed help with something, none had the money to pay her. The girl, being the sweet thing she was, helped each neighbor anyway.

As the story progresses, the girl begins to fret about her inability to earn the money she needs to buy the gift she wants for her mother, but as she helps each neighbor, the town begins to change. Those who lived in fear and isolation begin to emerge from their homes, and over time, the town, which had seemed to have settled into permanent darkness, begins to lighten.

In the end, the gift that the girl is able to give to her mother is not the trinket she hoped to buy, but a town filled with new hope for a brighter future. With her good deeds, she'd brought love and promise to a town that had lost its faith along the way.

I smiled as I set the book on the bedside table. This was exactly the message I needed as I headed into my day. Leave it to Gracie to know exactly what I needed to see, exactly when I needed to see it.

# Chapter 5

Gilda Frederickson lived in a lovely home on the south edge of town. When Mrs. Ewing lived in the house, she'd kept a lush garden, and I remembered that she always decorated for the holidays. I supposed the reason the house didn't display the lights I remembered had more to do with the medical issues of the woman who lived there now than anything else. I also supposed that a cold and snowy mountain home wasn't the best place for a woman in her late sixties or early seventies with a broken hip to winter. But knowing the residents of this small town, I was sure that Ms. Frederickson would have all the help she needed.

"Can I help you?" Asked a woman, who looked to be in her thirties, after answering the door.

"My name is Callie Collins. I'm here to see Gilda Frederickson."

The woman stepped aside. "My name is Hallie. I'm Ms. Frederickson's niece. She's been expecting you."

"Do you live here in town?" I asked.

"No. I'm just visiting. My mother sent me to check on Aunt Gilda. She was worried about her overall health after her fall, but she seems to be doing fine." Hallie opened a door at the back of the house. "Ms. Collins is in here."

Once Gilda acknowledged my presence, I handed her the muffins I'd brought. She thanked me, handed the muffins to Hallie with instructions to put them in the kitchen, and then Hallie left. "Thank you for meeting with me," I said to the woman in the wheelchair, who looked younger and healthier than I'd expected. Hallie seemed to be right about her aunt bouncing back quickly. "As I mentioned on the phone, I am writing a feature story about Secret Santa and wanted to ask about the gift you received."

"Of course. Please have a seat. I've read your column and have enjoyed it very much. I was particularly impressed that you managed to find the missing funds for the tree lighting. I think the whole town thanks you for that."

I sat down on the chair the woman pointed to. "It took some digging, but I was glad I was able to find the funds in time to get the tree lighting back on track."

"I understand that it was the town's bookkeeper who embezzled the money."

I nodded. "She never actually took the money, but she did move small amounts of money from a lot of different accounts into a new account within the system that only she had access to. She was pretty clever about the way she went about it. If not for the fact that she happened to take a larger than average percentage from the account that had been set aside for the town's tree lighting ceremony, she might have gotten away with it."

"Do you know why the woman did what she did?"

I crossed my legs and leaned forward just a bit. "I guess she'd been dealing with some medical issues and had gotten behind on her mortgage and several of her other bills. I suppose she might have felt desperate and decided to hide some money for future use if she needed it. I really don't condone what she did, but I do feel bad that the poor thing might end up spending Christmas in jail."

"Has she been arrested?"

"No. Not yet. The town has someone going over the books to confirm exactly how much she moved, and whether all of it is in the dummy account as she swears it is. I suppose it might help her case if the money is all there, and she is able to return it. Still, I doubt she'll get out of this without consequences of some sort. When I set out to find the missing funds, I had only the best of intentions, but now I feel sort of bad about the way things worked out."

"It is easier when the bad guys in our drama are actually bad and not simply desperate people making poor choices."

"Exactly." I smiled at the woman. "So about Secret Santa."

She looked me in the eye. "Before we begin, tell me a bit about yourself. I understand you are Gracie Hollister's niece."

I nodded. "Great niece. Aunt Gracie raised me after my parents were killed in an auto accident, so I grew up here. I remember your mother. I didn't know her well, but I do remember her lovely garden and her colorful holiday decorations."

"Mama did love the holidays." Her eyes softened. "She spent a lot of time and expended a lot of effort to make sure everything was just as it should be for each and every holiday and milestone when my sister and I were growing up. There isn't a day that goes by that I don't think of her and remember how she seemed to understand the importance of fully embracing each moment."

"That's really beautiful." It was times like this that I felt a little sad that I'd never have a daughter to remember me the way Gilda remembered her mother.

"I understand that you were a pianist before returning to Foxtail Lake," she continued.

"Yes." I flexed the fingers on my left hand. "I was injured in an accident and can no longer play at the level needed to continue with my career, so I decided to come home. To be honest, I hadn't planned to stay at first, but I find I am settling in quite nicely. Gracie told me that you worked with Hope."

She shifted her leg slightly and then answered. "I do, or at least I did before I ended up in this blasted contraption." She glared at the wheelchair. "I worked as a librarian before coming to Foxtail Lake to help my mother. After she recovered from her surgery, I went to work part-time for the local library. Eventually, I decided to retire, but I continued to volunteer at the library as well as other places around town. Of course, now that I am stuck in this chair, I guess I am stuck in the house as well. But you aren't here to listen to me complain. You want to hear about Secret Santa."

I wasn't sure what to say at this point. It was true that I was here to talk about Secret Santa, and I did have a schedule to adhere to, but it seemed rude to point that out when the woman wanted to chat. Making the decision to jump in now that I had an opening, I asked about the way the woman's Secret Santa gift had been delivered.

"I found a gift card for Smitty's Snow Removal in my purse. The gift card entitles me to unlimited snow removal for the entire season. Initially, I figured that Smitty had somehow slipped the gift card into my purse, but I asked him about it, and he said he hadn't. He told me that the gift card had been purchased by an anonymous source. Then I heard about the other folks in town who'd received Secret Santa gifts and figured that my benefactor was actually the jolly man in red."

"Do you know how the gift card got into your purse?"

She shook her head. "No idea. I figure that someone must have slipped it in when I was at church. Hallie has been helping with the shopping and other errands since she has been here, so I really don't have a reason to get out much, which is a good thing given my current circumstances, but I do have a neighbor who picks me up and takes me to church every Sunday."

"Was your purse out of your sight during services?" I asked.

"Briefly. I'd left my coat and purse in the pew during communion. I wasn't worried about it since I was in a church. I didn't think anyone would bother my personal possessions."

"So someone who was also at church on the day the gift card was delivered is most likely Secret Santa."

She shrugged. "I would imagine that to be a true statement."

I paused and considered the situation. "Did you ask anyone in the area if they'd seen who'd slipped the gift card into your purse?"

"No. I didn't even notice it until after I got home. I really have no idea who might have gifted me the snow removal, but I will say that I am extremely grateful that they did. There was no way I was going to be able to handle it myself."

I narrowed my gaze. "Had you handled it yourself in the past?" The woman looked to have been in good health before her fall, but she still seemed much too old to have shoveled her own snow even last year when she had two good hips.

"I've always shoveled my own walk. I have a service that does the driveway. I suppose if I hadn't been gifted the snow removal this season, I would have found a way to cut costs to pay for it myself, but now I can have clear walks and keep my cable for the winter. I'm very grateful for that."

"It was a thoughtful gesture," I agreed. "I don't suppose you have any idea who Secret Santa actually is?"

"Not really."

"But you must be curious."

"I guess I am curious, but I figure that if the person behind the gifts wanted to be identified, they would have left a card. I actually think the mystery as to Secret Santa's identity makes the whole thing a bit more magical. I mean, even as a kid, wasn't it the fact that Santa was a secret to wonder about but never to know that really drew you in?"

I supposed it was. I also supposed that it made sense that if Secret Santa had purchased the gift card from Smitty, then Smitty must know who Santa was. Maybe it made sense to add the individuals who had sold the goods to Secret Santa to my list of people to talk to.

"So of all the people in town that Secret Santa could have chosen to give a gift to, any idea why he chose you?"

She tilted her head slightly. "You think Secret Santa is someone I know. A friend, perhaps."

"It makes sense. Not only did he choose you to receive a gift, but he seemed to know exactly what gift you would appreciate the most."

"I guess you make a good point. But I know a lot of people in town, so I'm not sure that really narrows things down for you."

"No, I guess it doesn't."

"What I do know is that I was feeling sort of down and sorry for myself after my accident. I guess I let my bad mood affect me more than I should have, and I suppose I might have been letting that bad mood affect others. But then someone I may not even know did something wonderful. The gift of snow removal might seem small to some, but for me, it was a sign that there was still hope and goodness in the world. It meant someone was thinking of me and cared about my happiness. Until you are in the position of needing to rely on others, you really can't know how much a simple act of kindness can mean. Secret Santa gave me more than a gift card. He reminded me of the joy of the season, and for that more than anything, I am eternally grateful."

# Chapter 6

My next appointment was with Connie Denton. Secret Santa had given her a down payment on the diner where she'd worked as an employee for twenty years. I assumed the down payment on a diner would be a considerable amount of money, which made it seem even less likely that the transaction had been handled anonymously. Connie had suggested I come to the diner during the brief lull between the breakfast and lunch crowd, so timing my visit was important if I wanted her to have time to chat.

The Foxtail Diner had been in Foxtail Lake since there had been a town. I wasn't sure exactly how long the diner had been around, but I was pretty sure that Connie was at least the fourth or fifth owner. It was nice that she'd been able to buy the diner where she'd worked for so long. Cass had told me that she planned to leave the diner exactly as it had always been, menu and all. Everyone in town was happy that Connie had gotten the help she needed to buy the diner. An out of town buyer might have felt the need to change everything, and that wouldn't have gone over well with the town's residents, who seemed to appreciate tradition.

"Callie," Connie hugged me when I walked through the door. "I was so happy to hear that you were back."

"It's good to be back." I'd hung out at the diner, eating burgers and drinking shakes for most of my high school years. I'd meant to come in before this but somehow had never gotten around to it. "And congratulations on buying the diner."

Connie grinned. "Can you believe that Santa just gave me the down payment on this place? I mean, who would do something like that? When the loan officer, who by the way, had just turned me down for not having a down payment, called and told me that a down payment had been provided by an anonymous donor, I didn't believe him. I actually thought he was pulling my leg, and the whole thing was just some cruel joke. But he insisted that he was telling the truth and suggested I come down to discuss the loan now that the down payment obligation had been met. I was totally in shock. I'm still in shock. Very, very grateful, but utterly and completely in shock." She took me by the hand. "It's pretty slow right now. Let's grab a booth in the back, and we'll chat."

I let the woman, who I estimated to be in her early to mid-forties, drag me toward the back of the diner.

"It seems as if the Secret Santa gift was really a gift to the town as well as to you personally," I pointed out. "This place has a lot of history. Tradition. I understand business owners wanting to retire and move off the mountain, so I understand that businesses must trade hands from time to time, but if the diner had been sold to someone from out of the area, the history and tradition that is so important to the town could very well have been lost."

She raised her brow. "That's true. Personally, I don't plan to change a thing other than to add a special of the day, which I'll describe on the chalkboard near the front counter. That will allow me to experiment a bit with new dishes without having to change the menu."

"I think that is a wonderful idea." I looked around at the brightly decorated space. Carols played in the background, garland lined the counter, and the same train and miniature village that had graced the place when Gracie was a girl were still displayed. "So it sounds as if the money for the down payment was delivered directly to the bank."

She nodded. "I knew that buying this place was a longshot, but I also knew I had to try in spite of the fact I have about ten dollars in my savings account. I filled out an application for a loan, and quite frankly, I was assuming they would turn it down right away, but much to my surprise, I was assigned a loan officer. Randy Trainer. He is actually the only loan officer at the local bank, but he still took the time to help me through the process. He told me right up front that the odds of the bank giving me a loan with no down payment were slim to none, but he also reminded me that there was really nothing to be lost by trying. He got creative and assigned a value to my personal possessions, including my old clunker of a car. He figured that if we assigned a value and then used the value as collateral that might get the board to approve at my application, but it didn't work. Randy really did the best he could, but I had nothing to work with. He called and let me know that he'd done what he could, but that the bank wasn't going to bite. I'd accepted that, and then he called back to let me know that an anonymous donor had put up the down payment, and we were back in business."

"And he didn't tell you who put up the money?"

"He didn't tell me because he didn't know. Someone simply mailed in a cashier's check for the down payment along with specific instructions for its use."

"So, if you had to guess, who donated the money?" I asked as the song in the background changed from Rudolph the Red-Nosed Reindeer to Frosty the Snowman.

She narrowed her gaze. "I'm really not sure. I have thought about it. I mean, someone just gave me what amounts to a fortune in my book. There aren't a lot of people in the area with the means to do that. I figure the person who sent the money has to be local. Otherwise, how would they even know about my desire to buy the diner?"

"That's true. The donor is probably a local, and he or she is most likely someone who is known to you. I don't suppose you'd want to take a guess at who he or she might be?"

"Dean and Martin Simpson come in sometimes," Connie continued. "They certainly have the means to put up a down payment for this place if they wanted to, and they do seem to enjoy the food and the atmosphere. I suppose if I had to guess, I would say that the donor might have been them. As brilliant as they are, they are sort of set in their ways, and they did make a comment at one point about not wanting anything to change after it was sold."

Dean and Martin had been on my original list as well. Perhaps a conversation with the men was in order. I knew the pair were pretty reclusive, and I really didn't know them at all, but Cass was friends with the brothers, so perhaps I'd have him set up a meeting.

My other idea, in terms of identifying the guy, was to try to speak to Randy or someone at the bank. I understood that the cashier's check had been an anonymous donation, but there had been other Secret Santa gifts that had gone through the bank. Grover Wood had received cash on his behalf to bring his overdue mortgage current. Surely, someone at the bank had to have been in on the whole thing.

Of course, if someone had simply sent in a cashier's check with instructions as to where to apply it, then I supposed the staff at the bank might have been as clueless as anyone. I wondered if there was a way to track down the source of a cashier's check. Both the down payment for the diner and the paydown of the mortgage would have been large amounts. Surely, there would be a paper trail somewhere. I wasn't a financial wizard by any means, so maybe I'd ask Cass to help me find the information I was looking for.

"I guess you heard about Dennis Felton," Connie said after I'd let the conversation lull.

"Dennis Felton? Did he receive a gift from Secret Santa?"

"No. He was arrested."

I raised a brow. "Arrested?" I'd estimate Dennis was a man in his late sixties, who like Tom, tended to hang out at the lodge. He'd owned a local paint store for as long as I could remember. He was a nice guy whom everyone seemed to really like. I couldn't imagine what he'd done to get himself arrested. "What did he do?"

"I guess he punched Vern Tidwell in the face after Vern had a few too many drinks and started spouting off about the fact that Dennis and Buford had argued on the day Buford died, and he wouldn't be surprised if Dennis hadn't been the one to hit him over the head, causing him to pass out in the snow."

"So is the fact that Buford was hit in the head public knowledge?"

She shrugged. "I don't know if it is public knowledge, but Vern seemed to know about it. I guess now everyone knows about it. It makes sense that there was a reason that Buford froze to death. It never sat right with me that he simply drank too much and then passed out and froze to death. The man can pretty much drink anyone in town under the table. It would take a whole lot of alcohol to bring him to the point where he didn't even realize he was lying in the snow."

"Do you know what Dennis and Buford were arguing about on the day Buford died?"

She shook her head. "I'm not sure. Everything I know, I learned from folks who'd heard about Dennis's arrest and were chatting about it during breakfast. I suppose you can ask Cass if you are really interested."

"I will. I wonder if Cass plans to keep Dennis locked up, or if he plans to process and release him."

"I imagine it will be a catch and release situation. Dennis does drink too much at times, and he has punched a few faces, but all in all, he is a pretty good guy. I doubt Cass will keep him longer than he needs to in order to bring home the point that the guy needs to get help for his drinking and anger issues."

"I remember Dennis from when I lived here before. I know he was an adult, and I was a kid, but I don't remember him being a drunk."

"He wasn't," Connie informed me. "He didn't start drinking until after his wife died. I guess he never recovered from that."

Just about the time I figured I had the information I needed for my article, the lunch crowd began to arrive, so I thanked Connie and said my goodbyes. My last appointment of the day before I had to go and pick Paisley up from school was with Billy Prescott and his mother, Janice. Billy, who was a paraplegic, had received a new wheelchair after his mother had backed over his old one. The new one was not only a replacement but an upgraded model as well.

I'd never met either Billy or Janice, but Janice seemed willing to chat with me when I'd called and introduced myself. Like Gilda Frederickson, she'd read my columns and was excited about being featured in the next issue of the local newspaper and possibly even The Denver Post. Billy was homeschooled due to his difficulty getting around in the winter, so we agreed to meet at their home, which thankfully was not all that far from the elementary school where I would pick up Paisley.

After a brief introduction at the door when I arrived, Janice showed me to a room in the back of the house with windows that overlooked both the mountain and the valley.

"Wow. What a great view," I said, as I stood in front of the window.

"It is really exceptional, especially considering we are so close to town. Please have a seat on the sofa. Billy is in the den. I'll go get him and bring him in here. This is a much nicer room for us to have our chat."

I did as Janice suggested and took a seat looking out the large picture window. The view from the house I lived in with Gracie was pretty spectacular given the fact that it was right on the lake, but this view was so expansive as to take your breath away. There was something about a sky view that really opened things up. I could imagine sitting on this sofa and watching the storms roll in.

The interview with Janice and Billy lasted exactly thirty minutes. I learned that the new wheelchair had been delivered by an out of town service and that their records showed the shipper as being the store the new wheelchair had been ordered from. Janice informed me that she'd called the store that sold the wheelchair in an effort to find out who she should thank for their generosity, but was told that the purchase was made anonymously and they were not at liberty to provide her with any additional information.

So, in other words, I was back to square one. I did manage to get photos, quotes, and anecdotes for my story, so my interviews today were not a complete waste of time. Both Janice and Billy had been completely drawn in by the magic and the mystery of Secret Santa. When Billy's wheelchair had been damaged, they figured they'd need to use their savings to put a down payment on another one, which would make for a pretty bleak Christmas, but with the gift of the new chair, they shared that now they would be able to embrace the Christmas season as they always had. This year, Billy and his mom were busy making sweaters for the animals at the shelter. The sweaters, like the animals, came in all shapes and sizes, and each was unique. Janice shared that she'd taught Billy to knit when he was a small child stuck in a chair with nowhere to expend his energy. Both mother and son were really very good at their craft, and I was sure the animals at the shelter would enjoy the sweaters designed specifically for warmth.

While I was happy for Billy and his mother, I was disappointed they couldn't direct me to the person behind the gift. I had others to speak to, however. I figured I'd try to track down Donnie and Grover tomorrow, and then write my column over the weekend. I'd also start setting up interviews with prospective Secret Santas over the weekend. Maybe I'd even start my interviews this weekend. I wanted to speak to as many people as I could before my deadline for the second article in the series, so I'd have as many anecdotes to draw from as possible as I wrote it. Assuming, of course, that Dex liked my article about the recipients and let me continue with the series rather than turning it over to Brock.

# Chapter 7

## Friday

A quick glance out my bedroom window revealed the fact that the snow had paused at least for the moment. I was enjoying the beauty of the snowy landscape, but I did hope that it would be dry for the tree lighting this evening. Dealing with the cold was going to be hard enough, but if you threw in a heavy snow, the turnout was sure to be affected.

I rolled out of bed and turned on the lights I'd draped around my window. I wasn't sure why, but every time I looked at the lights, I found myself smiling. So far, this holiday season had been enchanting. Exactly the sort of thing I needed to chase away the last of the self-pity I'd been struggling with since my accident. Life, I decided, was pretty darn perfect. Paisley and I'd decorated the tree in the attic yesterday, and it had turned out amazing. Paisley has a natural eye for color and design, and the tree ended up looking like something you would find in a magazine. Not only did the tree look awesome, but we'd had a lot of fun as well. So much fun, in fact, that when Paisley had shared that her grandmother hadn't felt up to getting a tree, I'd taken her to the tree lot where we purchased two small trees for Paisley's grandmother's house, one for the living room, and one for Paisley's bedroom. After we set them up, we'd decorated both while Ethel offered decorating advice from the sidelines.

All in all, it had been a fun and relaxing afternoon. It had even gotten Paisley and Ethel talking about the idea of putting some carols on the stereo and baking a batch or two of the gingerbread cookies they'd baked in the past. I could see a glimmer of hope and energy in both their eyes. Having Paisley's mother ill for so long and then dealing with her death seemed to have been harder on them than I'd realized. I hoped now that the joy of the season had been introduced into their home, the pair would run with it and have the merriest of holidays in spite of their grief.

Today, I planned to track down both Grover Wood and Donnie Dingman. I'd need to finish the interviews for my column before my volunteer shift at the shelter. I planned to write the column this weekend, and then move onto the Secret Santa suspects as soon as I solidified a list of individuals to speak to. In the meantime, there was a wonderful smell coming from downstairs, so perhaps coffee and breakfast were the immediate order of the day.

"Morning, Aunt Gracie," I greeted as I poured myself a mug of coffee.

"Good morning, dear. How'd you sleep?"

"Really good, actually."

"I made cinnamon rolls if you're interested."

I poured a dollop of cream in my coffee. "I'm always interested in your cinnamon rolls. It seems like you've been baking a lot lately."

"Baking helps me to relax." She slid a roll from the pan onto a plate and handed it to me.

"Have you been stressed?" I asked, picking up on the subtle clue that baking relaxed her, and she'd been baking up a storm.

"Not really." She slid a roll onto a plate for herself. "Well, maybe a bit. But it is nothing I want you to worry about."

Well, now I was worried. "What's going on?" I asked in what I hoped was my most encouraging tone of voice.

"It's Nora. She's been diagnosed with cancer."

Nora Nottaway was one of Gracie's best friends. She was a few years younger than Gracie was but close enough in age that they'd always been friends. Both had lived in Foxtail Lake for their entire lives, and they shared a rich and vast history.

"Oh, no. I'm so sorry." I crossed the room and hugged Gracie. "Is it... Is she..." I was trying to find a way to ask if it was early and therefore treatable, or if it was only a matter of time.

"She is receiving treatment," Gracie answered, seeming to understand what it was that I'd been trying to ask. "I spoke to Ned this morning, and he seemed to think that Nora is doing just fine, given the circumstances."

Ned was Nora's husband. The couple owned and operated the general store.

"I'm really sorry to hear this. Is there anything I can do?"

"Pray. Nora had pneumonia last year, and I feel like she never really fully recovered from it. I will admit to being really worried whether or not her body has the strength to fight this."

"She seemed fine the last time I saw her."

"Nora always seems fine," Gracie answered. "She isn't the sort to want to share her struggles, which is why you can't share what I have told you with anyone else. She wants to keep this to herself for now. I shouldn't have said anything to you, but you were here, and I was feeling down after my conversation with Ned this morning. I guess I just needed someone to talk to."

I hugged the woman who meant so much to me. The woman who'd always been there for me. "Of course, you can count on me to keep Nora's secret. And any time you need to talk, I'm here for you. And, of course, I will include Nora as well as Ned in my prayers. If there is anything else I can do, you just need to ask."

"Thank you, dear. I appreciate that. So, what do you have planned for today?"

Gracie seemed to want to change the subject, so I answered. "I need to interview Grover Wood and Donnie Dingman about their Secret Santa gifts, and then I have my volunteer shift at the shelter. I'm assuming that you and Tom still plan to pick up Ethel and Paisley for the tree lighting?"

"We do."

"Great, then Cass and I will meet you there. We will probably stop somewhere for dinner after the tree lighting. You are welcome to join us unless it is too late for you."

"I think it might be too late for Ethel. We'll just bring them home after the tree lighting, and you and Cass can have your date."

I wanted to argue that what we were doing was eating and not dating, but it seemed pointless to bother at this point. Gracie knew how I felt about dating. It was the same way she felt. If you were a Hollister and a female, then everyone knew it was best to leave true love and happily ever after to others.

"You know, you might want to add Stephanie Baldwin to your Secret Santa list if you haven't already," Gracie said after a minute.

"Did Stephanie receive a Secret Santa gift?"

Gracie nodded. "Ned mentioned it this morning. I guess that Secret Santa had an oven and stovetop delivered to her home. The old one broke more than a month ago, and she couldn't afford to have it repaired or replaced, so she has been making do without one."

"That's really wonderful. I'll call her. I'd love to include her story in my article."

"I'm sure she'll be happy to chat with you. From what I understand, she has been telling everyone about her special gift."

I got up to refill my coffee mug. "This Secret Santa story has really turned into a big deal for Dex, and I really want to do a good job both for my own career and for Dex, who wants the expanded exposure, but I feel sort of bad that I am actively looking to unmask this man, or woman, who has done so much good for so many people."

"I suppose that is understandable. It occurred to me that if Secret Santa wanted to be identified, he, or she, wouldn't be going to so much trouble to remain anonymous."

"Exactly. But if I refuse to do the story, Dex will just have Brock write it, and Brock won't hesitate for a minute to unmask Secret Santa if it means a byline in the Post."

"So, what are you going to do?"

"I'm not sure," I said, furrowing my brow. "I feel really good about the story I am working on this week, so I guess I'll just finish it and then try to figure the rest out. I owe it to Dex to tell him if I am going to have a problem with the final article. I mean, if I really don't think I can write it, I guess I should let him put Brock on it right away. Dex has been so good to me. He has given me a part-time job even though I am in no way qualified to be a newspaper reporter. And if I am going to stay in Foxtail Lake for the long haul, which at this point is exactly what I plan to do, then I really want to earn more hours at the newspaper. I'm hoping Dex will like my work and actually hire me full-time, rather than just paying me as a columnist."

"It seems like you have a hard choice ahead of you."

I glanced out the window at the falling snow. "Yeah. I guess I'm going to have to give it some thought."

# Chapter 8

Grover Wood was a long-time local who'd lived in Foxtail Lake for as long as I could remember. He'd married his high school sweetheart, a very nice woman he'd been happily married to for twenty-five years before she passed away due to complications from diabetes. The couple never had children, but according to Aunt Gracie, who knew them better than I did, they'd always seemed happy with their lives in spite of the challenges presented. After Grover lost his wife, he threw himself into work, hobbies, and volunteer duty at the church and library. Most people felt that he was doing okay after the loss of his wife until he was seriously injured in a snowmobile accident this past winter, and the injuries to his back and neck left him unable to work.

I'd learned that Grover had burned through his savings after the accident, and was on the verge of losing his home when Secret Santa came to the rescue. I understood why the man was thrilled with the short reprieve but wondered if having his past debt erased and being paid up three months ahead would really help him in the long run. It seemed to me that what he really needed was a new source of income now that his days as a contractor seemed to have come to an end.

Gracie felt that the man had many talents that could be utilized to provide future income, but I guess the accident had destroyed more than his back; it had destroyed the last bit of hope and determination he'd been clinging to in the wake of his wife's death. I was by no means a psychologist, nor an expert on grief, but I suspected the man had been able to delay the normal mourning process after his wife passed as long as his life had been busy. But once he was laid up and forced to take some down time, everything he'd been holding together had come crumbling down around him.

Gracie had cautioned me to go easy on him during our interview, and I planned to take her advice to heart. I wanted to learn about his experience with Secret Santa, but I didn't want to push him over the edge I suspected he was still desperately clinging to.

"Grover Wood?" I asked the man who'd aged quite a bit since the last time I'd seen him, which was probably more than fifteen years ago.

"That's right. You must be Callie Collins. I remember you from church when you were a kid. Come on in." He stepped aside.

"Your view is lovely." I paused to admire the view of the mountains in the distance.

"I've always enjoyed it." He motioned for me to take a seat.

The house was clean and decorated fully for the upcoming holiday. I had to admit I wasn't expecting that. I guess I just assumed that a man suffering from loss and depression would have let things go. Of course, the man didn't look depressed. In fact, he looked downright cheerful. Perhaps I'd been wrong in my assessment of what was going on.

"So, you wanted to ask about Secret Santa?" he asked after I'd taken a seat.

"That's right. I understand that Secret Santa helped to bring your mortgage current."

"He did. And a lot more as well."

"Do you care to elaborate?"

"After my wife passed, I threw myself into my work, my sports, my hobbies, and even my volunteer work at the church and library. A busy body is a tired body, and a tired body doesn't have much energy to commit to feeling sorry for itself, so it all worked out for a while. But after my accident, when I was forced to stay home with nothing but my thoughts to keep me company, I guess I might have slipped into a bit of a depression. Things really were dark there for a while. Not only had I lost my source of income, but I'd also lost my hobbies and sports that kept me sane. What it really boiled down to was a loss of the defense system I'd created to help me deal with the loss of my wife."

"I'm so very sorry."

"No need to be. I realize now that trying to run from my grief wasn't the best approach anyway. I needed time to process everything, and I guess that my accident gave me the time I needed. Of course, by the time I began to dig myself out of my depression, I was in quite the financial mess. But then Secret Santa came along and gave me a second chance. One I plan to utilize to the fullest. I have a job interview next week, which I feel really good about, and once my mortgage was made current, the bank was willing to work with me on restructuring my other debt into something a bit more manageable."

"That's wonderful." I smiled. "I'm so happy to hear that things are back on track for you." I hated to ask my other questions since this seemed to be as good a place as any to end the interview, but then I remembered Dex. "Secret Santa really has been a ray of sunshine in the community. Everyone seems to have their own opinion as to who the mystery man might be. I don't suppose you'd care to wager a guess?"

"If I had to guess, I'd say Carolyn Worthington is my personal Secret Santa. Carolyn was friends with my wife, and Carolyn and I both volunteered at the library before I had my accident. Carolyn and I would sometimes have coffee after our volunteer shift, so I would say we know each other fairly well. I suspect that Carolyn somehow found out about my financial situation and decided to help out."

"So you think that Carolyn Worthington is behind all the Secret Santa gifts?"

He screwed up his face. "All the gifts? Well, I don't know about that. I suppose if she is the one to have helped me out, then it stands to reason that she is the one to help everyone out. I guess I never really stopped to look at the bigger picture." He paused, crossing his arms over his chest. "She is a bighearted woman. She is generous with both her time and her money. The idea that she found out about my situation and decided to help makes sense to me, but to be honest, I'm not sure about the others. Do you think there might be more than one Secret Santa?"

Did I? It would certainly complicate things, but I didn't suppose it was impossible that there was more than one Secret Santa out there.

After I spoke to Grover for a while longer, I headed across town to meet up with Stephanie Baldwin. As far as I knew, she'd been the most recent recipient of a Secret Santa gift. I hoped she might have some insight the others had been unable to provide.

As the others had, Stephanie showed me in once I arrived on her front porch. She led me down the hallway that smelled of chocolate and cinnamon and took me directly to her kitchen, where she positively beamed as she showed me her new oven, complete with an electric stovetop. It really was a nice unit. I wasn't much of a cook or really a cook at all, but I suspected the unit was good quality and featured all the bells and whistles.

"Isn't it fabulous?" She asked as she ran a hand over the surface of the cooktop. "Positively top of the line."

I looked at the dozens of cupcakes on the counter. "It looks like you have already put it to good use."

"Oh, I have. The cupcakes are for the tree lighting. The elementary school is doing a fundraiser, and the parents are supposed to donate baked goods to sell."

I wondered if Paisley was covered. I supposed I should call Aunt Gracie and ask her about it. Chances are if Paisley needed something to donate, Gracie would whip something up for her.

"So, how did you find out about your new oven?" I asked.

"The man from the appliance store called the house and asked me when it would be a good time to deliver and install the oven I'd ordered. I told him that he must have made a mistake since I hadn't ordered anything, but he was quite insistent. After a while, the guy was finally able to convince me that an individual who wanted to remain anonymous purchased the unit with instructions to deliver it to me."

"So, it sounds as if the man from the appliance store might know who paid for the oven."

She shrugged. "I guess, but he wasn't telling who it was, that much is for sure. Personally, I don't care who paid for it, I'm just happy to have it. This is the worst time of the year not to be able to bake anything. The school depends on me to bake treats for all their holiday parties, the town depends on my cookies and candy for the bake sale during Christmas in the Mountains, and my family depends on me to make all their favorite seasonal dishes. If you cook a lot as I do, it is important to have working equipment."

"I guess that is true. Do *you* have any idea who might have paid for the oven?"

The woman ran her hands down the front of her apron in what seemed to me to be a habitual movement. "If you're asking me if I know who Secret Santa is, I don't have a clue. And to tell you the truth, I don't care. Whomever the jolly elf in red is, the man is an angel in my book. A real hero sent to brighten the lives of the folks in town who need a little help making their miracle happen this Christmas." She paused for a breath and then continued. "I know a new oven might not seem like a lot to someone like you with your fancy career and truckloads of money, but to me, it is the difference between my ability to bake the Christmas cookies my children look forward to each year or going with store-bought. Not that there is anything wrong with store-bought mind you, but my cookies are one of the things I want my children to remember about me long after I'm gone. They're important, and I think Secret Santa knew that."

Fancy career and truckloads of money were far from an accurate description of me, but I did see what she was saying. "So, you suspect that Secret Santa is someone who knows you personally?"

"Well, I would think so. Otherwise, how would the man have known I needed an oven?"

Good question. A very good question, indeed.

# Chapter 9

As I did every Friday, I showed up for my volunteer shift at the animal shelter early so that I could work with the dogs currently going through the training class. The dogs I was asked to work with tended to rotate depending on which dogs needed extra practice, but the techniques used were much the same. When I'd first started as a trainer, the dogs tended to ignore my commands in favor of doing their own thing, but I'd learned a few tricks of my own along the way, and I felt I was beginning to get the hang of things.

"It seems like Koko has improved a lot in the past couple of weeks," Naomi commented after entering the room where I was taking the husky through his lesson.

"He does seem to be getting the hang of it," I agreed, as I motioned for him to sit and then stay. "It was rocky in the beginning, but I feel like the two of us understand each other at this point. Any luck finding someone to adopt him?"

"Actually, I do have a man who is interested. I'm not quite ready to let Koko go, but I did process the guy's application, and it seems like he might be a real possibility. If Koko does well this week, I think I'll set up an appointment for the dog to spend some time with the man to make sure they are compatible. It will be important that Koko respects whoever adopts him since he has such a dominant personality."

"I hope it works out. I'd love to see him in a real home for the holiday."

"That is my goal, as well. I'd love to get as many animals placed as possible, but we are already into December, so I'm not sure how many I'll be able to place. But not to worry, the dogs and cats who will spend the holiday at the shelter will be given special treats to celebrate."

"I agree that it's better to find the right home than to rush it."

"That has been my philosophy from the beginning. Is Cass coming today?"

I rewarded the dog and then asked him to lie down. "He is. At least that is the plan. I spoke to him earlier, but he got a call while we were chatting. He said he had to go and would call me later, but I haven't heard from him. The plan we worked out was to play with the dogs until about five-thirty and then head over to the tree lighting."

Naomi opened a cupboard and began sorting vitamin bottles. "I forgot that was tonight."

"I'm hoping there is a decent turnout. First, it was canceled, and then it was back on. I'm sure that there will be some folks who might not know things were worked out, and that the event is going to happen. And then there is the weather. It's positively frigid."

Naomi laughed. "That's a Rocky Mountain winter for you. The secret to surviving is layers. Lots and lots of layers."

"Thanks, I'll remember that."

She closed the cabinet. "Hancock is waiting for me over at the house, so I guess I should get back. Maybe I'll see you at the tree lighting. Hancock is flying out in the morning, and I want to hang out with him while I can, so I guess I'll see what he wants to do."

"He's leaving before Christmas?"

She shrugged. "He may be back by Christmas. Sometimes he is only gone for a week or two, while other times, it is a month or two, but I try not to have any expectations. That way, I'm not disappointed. I guess it will work out however it works out. If Cass does make it, can you ask him to stop by the house? I have the information on Rupert he was looking for."

"Rupert?"

"Rupert Wooly. He's an old prospector I've known forever. Like Hancock, he tends to come and go with the wind, but according to Cass, he happened to have been in town when Buford died, so Cass wants to chat with him."

"So, did he know anything?"

Naomi shrugged. "My assignment was just to track the guy down. I'll leave it to Cass to interview him."

I had to hand it to Naomi, she was about as easy going as anyone I'd ever met. She obviously cared deeply about the animals in her care, but beyond that, it seemed like she just drifted with the current going wherever it might take her. I supposed that was a good quality to have, but I was sure that simply floating through life without really needing to take control was something I would never be able to do no matter how hard I tried.

By the time I finished my training duties, Cass had shown up. I passed along the information that Naomi wanted him to come up to the house, and then I began gathering balls and toys for the play session. It was really gratifying to see how excited the dogs became once they realized that Cass and I were there to entertain them.

"So, did you get the information you needed?" I asked Cass after he returned from speaking to Naomi.

"I did. I'm not sure that Rupert will know anything, but he tends to hang out with the other old-timers that can usually be found at the bar, so I figured it couldn't hurt to talk to him. I've spoken to everyone else I can think of but, while everyone has an opinion as to what might have happened on the night Buford died, no one seems to actually know anything."

"It sounds frustrating."

"It has been."

"Did you speak to Ford?"

He nodded. "I did speak to Ford. Tom wasn't wrong when he said that Ford has been acting oddly. He was polite when I showed up at his home. He invited me in and even offered me some really bad coffee. I asked about his health since his house was a total mess, and it looked like he hadn't cleaned up in weeks. He said he was fine. Tired, but fine. I asked him if he knew anything about Buford's death, and he said he didn't, but I'm not sure he was telling the truth."

"Why do you say that?"

"He lowered his eyes when I brought up Buford's name. He answered my questions, but the entire time we were speaking about Buford, he stared down at the floor. I even asked him point-blank if he had something he needed to tell me. He said he didn't, but like I said, he just wasn't himself."

I furrowed my brow. "Do you think Ford killed Buford?"

"Intentionally and with premeditation, no. But Ford and Buford did get into it at times. I have to admit that by the time our conversation was over, I found myself wondering if Ford and Buford hadn't engaged in a tussle that led to Buford's death."

"Do you think Ford would lie about that if he had killed Buford?"

He shrugged. "I'd like to think he wouldn't, but I suppose if he is scared enough about the consequences of his actions, he might lie to protect himself."

I supposed Cass had a point. "So, what are you going to do?"

"Just keep an eye on him. I don't have a single lick of evidence that Ford killed Buford, so it's not like I can bring him in or ever get a warrant to search his place. But I can watch him and see what he does next. If Ford is guilty, I suspect he'll slip up at some point, and when he does, I'll be there to bring him in."

I tossed a thick rope for the dog who had brought it to me. "So, do you have any other suspects?"

"A few."

"I heard that you arrested Dennis Feldman for fighting with Vern Tidwell after Vern accused Dennis of being the one to hit Buford over the head."

He nodded. "That's true. I did have to arrest Dennis for punching Vern, but what I found the most interesting is that Vern knew that Buford died from a blow to the head. Neither the mayor nor the sheriff's office has made that fact public yet, so how did Vern even know that was what happened?"

"I had the same thought. It occurred to me that Vern accused Dennis of hitting Buford to divert attention from himself, but in reality, all he did was bring attention to his own actions. Have you spoken to Vern?"

"I have. He swears that he didn't kill Buford. He swears that he heard about Buford being hit over the head during a discussion with a group of guys at the bar. I suppose that might be true, word does tend to get around in a small town, especially with the bar crowd, but I'm keeping my eye on Vern as well as Ford."

"And Dennis?" I asked.

"Dennis told me that he and Buford did argue on the evening he died, but he swears he went to his girlfriend's house directly after the argument. I checked with the girlfriend, who lives in Aspen, and she confirmed that Dennis was with her for the entire night and into the following day."

"So, it sounds like Dennis is in the clear. Is there anyone else on your list besides Ford and Vern?"

"I have one other lead, and it might actually turn out to be a good one."

"And what is that?"

"Darby Willis told me that Buford recently inherited a pretty good chunk of change from his sister after she passed away this past summer. Darby didn't know how much Buford had inherited, but he was pretty sure it was a significant amount, whatever that means. The really interesting thing about this inheritance is that Buford and his sister, Hilde, were estranged, and as far as Darby knew, the two hadn't spoken in forty years."

"It seems odd that the woman would leave money to a brother she hadn't spoken to for all that time."

"I thought so as well, so I did a little digging. It turns out that Hilde has a son who was expecting to inherit her entire estate. When the son, whose name is Jason, found out that his mother gifted more than a quarter million dollars to his uncle, a man he'd never met, before she died, he retained an attorney and tried to challenge the gift."

"Why would she do that?"

"She'd been ill. I think she knew that she only had a matter of days or maybe weeks to live, so she went ahead and gifted the money to her brother. Maybe she knew her son would challenge the gift, so she wanted to head him off. It's hard to say."

"So, what happened when the son challenged the gift?"

He was successful in getting a judge to agree to temporarily freeze the account his mother had put the money into after making the case that his mother was dying and not in her right mind when she made the gift. When the court attempted to freeze the account, they found that there was only a hundred dollars left. Apparently, the bulk of the money had been withdrawn the day after Hilde gifted it to Buford."

"So, Buford must have anticipated a problem and withdrew the money."

Cass nodded. "Apparently. The thing is that no one has been able to figure out what he did with the money. He didn't open additional bank accounts, nor does it appear he made any investments, at least not any that can be tracked. He hasn't made any large purchases, nor was the money found in his house after he died."

"I didn't really know Buford, but based on what I've heard, it seems like he was the sort of guy who might have stuffed the money in his mattress."

"He was totally that sort of guy," Cass agreed. "But we've looked in the mattress, and in the root cellar, and even in the oven. The money simply is not on his property."

I had to admit the fact that Buford had come into a significant amount of money before he died did lend an interesting twist to the situation. "Okay, so if Buford had the money at his home at one point and someone found out about it, maybe someone killed him and stole the money."

Cass tossed a thick rope for the dogs to chase. "I suppose that is as good an explanation as any, but there are still a lot of unanswered questions, beginning with why this woman left such a large amount of money to a brother she'd been estranged from for forty years."

"That does seem odd," I agreed.

"And even if we can figure that out, we need to figure out why Buford withdrew all the money from the bank, and what he did with it once he liquidated."

"And, of course, you'll want to know if all of this is related to his death."

"Exactly."

I squatted down to greet a pair of terriers. "Have you spoken about the money to the people who were closest to Buford? Had he told anyone about his inheritance?"

Cass began picking up the toys in anticipation of wrapping up the play session. "I just found out about this today, so I've only had time to speak to a couple of Buford's friends. Those I've spoken to swear they had no idea that Buford had come into any money. As I already mentioned, after he withdrew the cash, it seems to have simply disappeared. Buford didn't change his lifestyle, nor did he make any large purchases."

"So, if someone killed Buford in such a way as to make it look like an accident and then stole the money as we've speculated, who even knew about it to carry out that plan?"

"That is a very good question."

I stood up, crossing my arms over my chest. "What about the nephew, Jason? We know he knew about Buford's inheritance, and we know he was unhappy that his mother left all that money to her brother rather than to him. We know he tried to freeze the account that was left to Buford, but the money was already gone. What if he came to Foxtail Lake to confront Buford, and when he got here, he found all that money just stuffed in a drawer in Buford's home? Could he be the one who killed him and then took off with the money he considered to be his in the first place?"

"I think that is a good possibility. I've been trying to track the guy down. He lives in Denver, so I may have to have the Denver PD go to his house and talk to him. I guess I'll see if he calls me back."

"And in the meantime?"

"In the meantime, I'm going to speak to Rupert now that Naomi has tracked him down for me, and I plan to continue to dig around in the memories of the guys who hang out at the bar and the lodge. I've got someone looking for money or correspondence relating to an offshore account, but to be honest, money in a mattress seems more Buford's style than something as sophisticated as an offshore account."

"Based on what I've heard about the guy, I agree. Are you going to be able to go to the tree lighting with me?" I asked.

He nodded. "I've been looking forward to it all day. Do we need to pick up Gracie?"

"Aunt Gracie and Tom are picking up Ethel and Paisley. They're going to meet us there. I thought maybe we could get something to eat after."

"That sounds good. I'm starving. The actual tree lighting only lasts fifteen to twenty minutes. There are a few speeches, the tree is lit, and then everyone sings a couple of carols. Still, it can be crowded, and parking is an issue at times, so I suppose we should head in that direction."

"Should we tell Naomi that we're leaving?"

"Based on my observation when I went up to the house to talk to Naomi, I think she and Hancock might be busy. We'll lock up, but I don't think we need to bother them."

I called the dogs and headed toward the kennels. "Naomi said that Hancock is leaving again tomorrow."

"That's what Naomi indicated to me as well. I guess that is the package that comes with his job. It's not a lifestyle I would enjoy, but it seems to work for him. Did you already fill out the training log?"

"I did. I think we're good to go once we return everyone to the kennel."

After being exercised, the dogs seemed happy to return to their beds, where they had plenty of fresh water. I had to hand it to Naomi; she seemed to know exactly what needed to be done to ensure that each animal in her care was as happy and healthy as they could be in the absence of a special human that belonged only to them. There were times when I considered adopting one of the dogs, but I wasn't sure how Gracie and Alastair would feel about that. Volunteering allowed me to spend time with the dogs without making a long-term commitment. Then I would see how Milo and Cass interacted, and I'd find myself envying the bond they seemed to share with each other. The relationship between a man or woman and their dog really is a pretty special thing. Of course, the relationship I had with Alastair was pretty special as well, and I liked the fact that he was independent most of the time, but in the end, he was Gracie's cat. Maybe one day, I'd want to have a pet who was just mine.

# Chapter 10

## Monday

"This is good. Really good," Dex said after reading the column I'd just turned in that featured the recipients of the Secret Santa gifts. "This is exactly what I was looking for. Something personal. Something that really brings home the effect the gifts have had on the lives of those they've been bestowed upon."

I let out the breath I'd been holding. "Great. I'm really glad you like it. I worked hard on the interviews and the write-up. I really wanted to give you the story you were after."

"Well, you seem to have accomplished your goal."

I smiled, encouraged by his positive response. "So, about the second article, the one featuring the Secret Santa prospects. Am I cleared to run with it as well?"

He hesitated. "Writing the second article is also supposed to serve the purpose of gathering the information you are going to need for the third article... the big reveal. Do you really think you are up for that?"

Did I? Honestly, I wasn't sure. I wanted to assure Dex that he had nothing to worry about, but I knew how important this series was to him and didn't want to be the one to let him down. "I have some good leads," I answered. "And I'd really like the chance to see where they take me."

Dex puckered his lips. "You did a good job this week, and I want to reward that by allowing you to continue, but I have a lot riding on this. I need you to be certain you can see it through."

There was a part of me that wanted to take the easy way out and tell him to give the story to Brock, but if I ever wanted a staff position, I knew I needed to step up and do what needed to be done. Besides, Calliope Rose Collins wasn't a quitter. I would never have been able to reach the heights I had as a musician if I'd allowed myself to quit every time things got tough. I knew that if you wanted to make your dreams come true, you had to clutch onto those dreams and never let go. "I can get you what you need," I said with more confidence than I felt. "I have some strong leads, and I promise I will follow them wherever they might take me. You can count on me."

"Okay. The series is yours. I look forward to the next two articles."

"Thank you so much for this opportunity. I won't let you down."

"You are most welcome." Dex got up and refilled his coffee mug. "How was your weekend?"

"It was really nice. The tree lighting was lovely. I forgot how much I used to enjoy it when the whole town came together to celebrate. It was cold, that's for certain, but really, really pretty."

"I got some great photos for this week's edition. I think I have one with you and Cass and Paisley in Santa's sleigh."

I smiled softly at the memory. "We did take a sleigh ride. When Paisley first asked about it, I was afraid it was going to be much too cold, but there was a warm blanket in the sleigh, and the man who ran the ride gave us hot cocoa. The ride went through town, so we could enjoy the decorations and then through the forest, so we could experience that as well. The trail through the forest was lined with white lights, which reflected off the snow like millions of little diamonds. It was magical."

"I don't suppose you want to write up a small feature about your experience to go with my photos."

I paused. "When would you need it by?"

"The end of the day."

I slowly bobbed my head. "Okay. The memory of that special evening is actually pretty fresh in my mind. If you have a computer I can use, I'll write something up right now."

He clapped his hands together. "Great. There is a computer on the desk in the front office."

I picked up my stuff. "Okay. I'll take care of it before I leave."

After I sat down at the desk, I took a minute to take it all in. To this point, I'd written the features that had been printed on my laptop at home, but working at an ink-smeared desk in a real newspaper office felt totally different. I actually felt like a real reporter for the first time. I had to admit the feeling was one I liked quite a lot. There was something about the scent of the place and the subtle noises in the background as various machines hummed and whirred. I don't remember ever wanting to be a journalist, but as I sat at the desk in the middle of the bullpen, I had the sense that I was really home.

"Did Dex finally give you a desk?" Gabby asked after walking in from somewhere down the hallway.

"No. I stopped by to turn in my Secret Santa story, and he asked me if I could write a feature about the tree lighting. He just wanted something short to go with the photos he took, so I told him I would write something up while I was here."

She sat on the corner of the desk. "So how'd Dex like the piece you wrote on Secret Santa?"

"He liked it. He is going to let me run with the rest of the series."

"That's wonderful." Gabby leaned forward slightly. "I might have a piece of information to share."

I leaned in even further. "Do tell."

"One of the women who goes to the same gym I do, told me that she heard from her hairdresser that Carolyn Worthington received a large shipment of flowers from a wholesale place in Denver and then the very next day, the church received an anonymous donation of red and white flowers for their advent service."

"So, Carolyn received an order of red and white flowers?" I asked.

"Actually, the woman I spoke to didn't know if the flowers Carolyn ordered were red and white. They came in boxes, so there is no way to know if they are the same flowers that were donated to the church. And even if Carolyn did donate the flowers, that doesn't necessarily mean that she is Secret Santa since a donation of flowers to a church is a whole lot different than making a down payment for someone on a restaurant, but I still thought it was worth mentioning."

"It was, and thank you. Carolyn is on my list of people to talk to, so I'll try to make a point to ask her about the flowers."

Once I completed my piece about the tree lighting, I turned it in to Dex and then headed toward the bank. I needed to identify Secret Santa, so even though I wasn't overly confident that the people at the bank would or could tell me what I needed to know, starting with the individuals who'd processed Connie's loan and Grover's mortgage payment seemed as good a place as any to start. After that, I supposed I'd start figuring out a way to run into my main Secret Santa suspects. Carolyn was in town often, so she wouldn't be too hard to corner, and Dean and Martin were friends with Cass, so I could ask him to arrange a meeting with them. Haviland Hargrove's name had been brought up, although I doubted he was Secret Santa. Still, he was usually hanging out at the lodge or at the bar, so I figured I could track him down fairly easily.

Once I arrived at the bank, I asked to speak to Randy Trainer. I'd never met Randy, but I figured I could pretend to be interested in a loan of some sort, and then once the ice was broken, ask what I was really here to ask. I planned to jump in by asking about Connie's down payment and then segue into a discussion about Grover's mortgage.

"Can I help you?" one of the women behind the teller's counter asked. There were two women at the counter today, but there were windows to accommodate three.

"Yes. My name is Calliope Collins. I'd like to speak to Mr. Trainer if he is available." I glanced toward the hallway, which featured doors to several offices.

"I'll see if he is available. Have you spoken to Mr. Trainer previously?"

"No. This is the first time. I grew up in Foxtail Lake but moved away after high school. I've only recently moved back."

"Of course. You must be Gracie's niece."

"Yes. That's right. Do you know my aunt?" Of course, she knew Gracie. It was a small town. Everyone knew Gracie.

"I do. She was already a customer when I started working here. Please have a seat, and I'll check with Mr. Trainer."

The waiting area was small but really nice. There were several long sofas arranged in a U-shape, which framed a river rock fireplace. The nearby picture window looked out onto a wooded area. As far as bank waiting areas that I'd been in, this was by far the nicest. The fire was warm and cheery. I was sure customers here on actual business would find that the pleasant atmosphere at least partially helped with any stress they might be experiencing.

"Mr. Trainer will see you now," the woman said. "Please follow me."

I stood up and ran a hand down the front of my thick forest green sweater. The sweater was nice, but glancing down at the rest of my attire, I realized I probably should have worn something a bit nicer than faded jeans and heavy snow boots. Of course, this was Foxtail Lake, and folks tended to dress down even if they were applying for a loan, which in reality, I wasn't.

"Ms. Collins," Trainer came out from behind his desk to shake my hand. "How can I help you today?"

"Honestly? I'm here to talk to you about Secret Santa. I spoke to Connie Denton, and she gave me your name. I understand you were helping her with her loan for the diner when Secret Santa provided the down payment."

The man motioned for me to take a chair. "Yes. That is correct."

"Connie told me that you received a cashier's check, which was sent to you anonymously, along with a note letting you know where to apply the money."

"Yes, that is correct, as well."

I crossed my legs and leaned forward just a bit. "I don't suppose you have any idea as to the source of the check?"

The man paused and then answered. "As you've already indicated, the check was delivered anonymously. I did verify that it was legitimate before depositing it into an escrow account, but I really can't tell you any more than that."

"Because you don't know more or because you aren't at liberty to say?"

"Both actually. I honestly don't know who sent the check, but even if I did, I wouldn't tell you or anyone for that matter. I'm sure you understand that all banking transactions are confidential."

I did understand that and was even expecting that response, but I figured I had to ask.

"And Grover Wood's mortgage? Was that also caught up by an anonymous donor?"

"The fact that you are asking indicates to me that you know it was. Is there a particular reason you are asking these questions?"

I knew it was a bad idea to tell the man I was researching a story, but it was the truth, and if he didn't know that now, he would figure it out when tomorrow's newspaper came out. "I am writing a series of articles for the newspaper about Secret Santa. The first article about the recipients of the Secret Santa gifts will come out tomorrow. I am currently researching the gift giver. There are a lot of opinions out there as to who Secret Santa might actually be, so tracking down the person responsible for all the generous gifts won't be easy. It occurred to me to ask those people who received the money from Secret Santa in exchange for goods and services for others, or in this case, in exchange for help with individual loans."

He leaned his elbows on the desk. "I see. I can't fault you for your logic, but as I've already said, I really can't help you."

I stood up. "Thank you for your time. I guess I knew you probably couldn't help me, but I had to try."

"Why are you trying to unmask Secret Santa anyway?"

"Like I said, I'm writing a series of articles."

He tilted his head slightly. "I know what you said, but why are you taking that approach. It seems to me that Secret Santa is a good person who is doing a good thing for the community and wants to remain anonymous. Why not let his identity remain a secret? I would think that if you simply focus on the recipients of the gifts and the positive effect those gifts have made on their lives, you will have plenty to write about."

"Actually, I agree with you. The problem is that my boss wants to publish a tell-all. I really love my job, which by the way, I'm brand new at, and therefore I really want to do a good job for him."

"I understand. Good luck with your story."

"Thank you. And again, thank you for taking the time to speak to me."

After I left the bank, I slowly drove through town toward the library. I needed to refocus, and I figured spending a few minutes chatting with Hope would help me to accomplish that. Hope Mansfield had been the librarian in Foxtail Lake since I'd been in high school. I figured she knew most of the people in town, and I knew from experience that she had a good head on her shoulders.

I waved to a group on the side of the road who were hanging wreaths on all the lampposts. Most of the town had been decorated before the tree lighting, but for some reason, perhaps the weather, the wreaths had been left for this week. I knew that the mayor and the entire event committee wanted to make sure everything was perfect before the huge Christmas in the Mountains event this upcoming weekend. Most of the store windows in town featured magical Christmas scenes, and the now barren trees along Main had been strung with white lights, so I figured once the wreaths were hung and the stop signs wrapped with red and white paper to make them look like candy canes, the merchants would be ready for the throngs of people they hoped would make the trip up from the valley next weekend.

"Morning, Hope," I greeted after entering the cheerily decorated library. "I love your tree. I didn't notice it on Saturday when I was here for the volunteer meeting."

"I didn't decorate it until after closing on Saturday."

"What made you think about hanging books on it?"

"This is a library. The paperbacks were donated to sell at our next fundraiser, but I figured I could use those with Christmas themed covers to brighten up the tree. What brings you out on this frosty winter morning?"

"Secret Santa." Then I explained the series of articles Dex wanted to run and my part in the whole thing.

"Wow. That's a tough assignment. Personally, I think most folks in town prefer that Secret Santa remain a mystery."

"Yeah," I blew out a breath. "I'm beginning to get that idea. I don't think pursuing Secret Santa's identity is going to win me any popularity contests, but Dex is my boss, and this series is a big deal to him. I really want to do a good job."

"Maybe you can talk him into doing the series without the big reveal at the end. I would think that the local paper would want to keep the secret as much as anyone."

"I think Dex has been swayed by the idea that the series is going to be featured in The Denver Post, and the guy from the Post wants a big reveal as the cherry on the top of the series. If not for the whole thing with the Post, I do think I might be able to convince him to skip the big reveal."

Hope twisted her lips to the side, making it appear as if she was conflicted about something.

"Do you think I should bow out and let Dex assign Brock to the remainder of the series?" I asked.

"Perhaps," she answered. "I do get the fact that this series could really help the career you didn't even know you wanted and really haven't even got off the ground yet, but the fallout from the public might be really brutal. Especially if the reveal makes Secret Santa angry and he or she stops doing good deeds in the community."

"Yeah, that did occur to me. The big reveal isn't going to be published until Christmas Eve, so chances are that he or she will be finished with the gift giving anyway, but still, I have to admit it doesn't feel right. And part of me really wants to fail at my assignment and keep the secret safe. But if I don't figure out who Secret Santa is, Dex will lose faith in me, and we are just getting started. I'd really hate to lose the progress I seem to be making."

"I get it. I do. I suppose all you can do at this point is do the job assigned to you and see how it all ends up. In the meantime, try to relax and enjoy the season. I can literally see you tensing up, and if you continue down that path, you are going to end up missing all the fun. Did you see the reindeer display they set up in the park?"

"Reindeer display? Are we talking real reindeer?"

She nodded. "Supposedly borrowed from Santa himself. The reindeer will be there until after the weekend, but you might want to stop by before the weekend if you are interested. I have a feeling the display is going to attract more than its share of spectators."

"Thanks for letting me know. I'll check them out."

"Did Gracie ever talk to you about the Santa House in the Village?"

"No. What is going on with the Santa House?"

"After we looked at everything everyone had signed up for at the meeting on Saturday, we realized we were still really short of volunteers for the Santa House. Mostly, we need elves."

"And what do the elves do?"

"Basically the elves handle crowd control. They make sure the line runs smoothly and help the little ones onto Santa's lap. That sort of thing. Gracie was going to ask if you'd be willing to give it a try, but she must not have gotten around to it yet."

I glanced suspiciously at Hope. "I have a feeling there is something you aren't telling me. Otherwise, it seems you would have plenty of volunteers for a gig such as that."

"Well, there is a costume to consider."

"Costume?"

"Basically, it consists of green tights and a red sweater. It really only works for those with a particular body type."

I looked down at my own body. "Thin and short."
"Exactly."

# Chapter 11

Hope, who knew Carolyn Worthington quite well, offered to call her and set up an appointment between the two of us. Carolyn wasn't busy today, so Hope arranged with me to meet with her within the hour. Carolyn was a rich woman before moving to Foxtail Lake. When she'd chosen the area to be her new home, she'd looked for a large parcel of land on a lake where she could build her mansion. I'd never had the opportunity to meet Carolyn or to visit her home to this point, so even though I was expecting vast luxury, I was truly amazed at how vast and luxurious her estate was.

After parking in the circular drive, I rang the bell and was greeted by a woman dressed in black and white. I was escorted into a room, which I assumed was a parlor of sorts, and asked to wait. After a few minutes, a woman dressed in riding clothes emerged from the hallway.

"Callie Collins?"

I stood. "Yes. I'm Callie."

"I'm Carolyn Worthington. I understand you want to speak to me about Secret Santa."

I nodded. "Yes. That is correct. I'm doing an article for the newspaper."

"Normally, I don't do interviews, but Hope speaks highly of you, so I decided to make an exception. I was just about to exercise my stallion. If you'd care to join me, we can chat while we ride."

"Ride?"

She slapped her riding gloves across her palm. "You do ride, don't you?"

I shook my head. "I'm sorry. No. In fact, I'm pretty sure I've never been on a horse in my entire life."

She looked me up and down. "You're dressed fine for the task, and I have a gentle mare that needs exercise. I'm sure you'll do fine."

"But…"

"Don't worry. We'll take it easy."

I was trying to figure out how I was going to get out of there when a man poked his head in through the doorway.

"Your ride is here," he informed Carolyn.

"Wonderful." She looked at me. "Are you ready?"

Ready? Was she kidding? I was here to interview the woman not to break my neck.

I frantically tried to come up with a plausible reason why it might be a better idea to simply wait for Carolyn to be freed up rather than to join her on her ride, but I was so terrified I couldn't speak. A man, also dressed in black and white, picked us up in a vehicle that looked like an enclosed golf cart. It must have had four-wheel-drive since I noticed it moved along just fine over the hard-packed snow on the drive.

The small vehicle pulled up in front of a large building which, I was soon to learn, was an indoor arena. Apparently, Carolyn loved to ride, and she'd built the facility so she could safely work her horses even in the dead of winter. She must have called ahead and let them know she had a guest because the man who met us was leading two very tall horses.

"This is Gaia." She introduced me to the horse I would be riding. "She is very gentle, and she knows exactly what to do. Really, you just need to climb up and hang on."

I looked at the horse, who was quite a bit taller than I was. "Climb up?"

"Brantley will show you to the mounting platform."

Carolyn took the reins of the second horse and accepted a small boost from Brantley, who then led the horse I was going to ride over to a set of stairs leading to a small platform. Once I climbed up onto the platform, I just needed to swing one leg over, and I would be sitting on the monster who I was sure was going to toss me onto the track once she figured out that I had absolutely no idea what I was doing. I swallowed and considered my options. I could run screaming from the building, but that wasn't going to get me the interview I wanted. My only choice was to throw caution to the wind, toss my leg over the saddle, and then hang on for dear life.

I held my breath as my backside settled on the saddle. The horse didn't move an inch. Okay, so far, so good. I had no idea what to do at this point. Brantley handed me the reins and schooled me to hold them gently. According to the man, who I imagined was some sort of handler, Gaia would follow along with Carolyn, so there was no need for me to do anything. I certainly hoped that was true because in this moment, doing nothing was really the only option I had.

"Just let Gaia take the lead," Carolyn advised as the horse began to walk.

I nodded as I held onto the saddle with both hands. I was holding my breath so I really couldn't speak at that point. At first, I was absolutely terrified, but after a minute or two, I began to rock with the rhythm of the horse beneath me and no longer felt quite as certain that I was going to die. It helped that Gaia didn't need to receive instructions. She seemed to know what to do and simply did it.

"So, what is it you want to ask me?" Carolyn asked once both horses had settled into a slow stroll around the arena.

I let out the breath I'd been holding, took in another, and answered. "As Hope told you, I'm working on a series of articles featuring Secret Santa."

"Yes. She did mention that."

"One of the angles I am looking at is the man or woman behind Secret Santa. Who is this person? Why are they anonymously bestowing what, in many cases, are very substantial gifts to the residents of Foxtail Lake?"

"And you think I might be Secret Santa?"

"I have a list of several prospects who have the financial means to be Secret Santa." I looked around at the private arena, which was larger than a city block. "Obviously, you fit that description."

She smiled. "Yes, I do have the financial means to be Secret Santa, but I'm afraid I'm not. I do love what this man or woman is doing. I give away quite a lot of money myself each year, but it never occurred to me to have so much fun doing it. The whole Secret Santa thing is really pretty ingenious."

"So you didn't pay up Grover Wood's mortgage? He said that you were friends."

"Grover and I are friends, and if I'd known how much trouble he was in, I would have gladly helped him out. But the thing is, Grover didn't confide in me. I knew he'd been in an accident, and I did take care of some of his medical bills that he probably doesn't even know I paid, but I didn't know about his situation with the bank and his mortgage. I guess I should have done more to check in with him after the accident. Once he was laid up, and I no longer ran into him around town, checking in with him sort of slipped my mind."

Well, that was disappointing. "And the flowers for the church?"

"What about them?"

"Did you donate them? I understand you received a large shipment of flowers right about the time someone donated a bunch of flowers to the church."

She laughed. "I did buy flowers, but they are for a cocktail reception I am throwing tomorrow evening. I didn't donate the flowers to the church, nor would I have done so. I give a cash donation to the church each month, so as far as I'm concerned if they really needed flowers, they could have used some of the cash I donated to buy them."

"So you didn't buy Billy Prescott a new wheelchair or Stephanie Baldwin an oven?"

"I did not."

"And you didn't help Connie Denton buy the diner or provide for snow removal for Gilda Frederickson?"

"I'm afraid not."

I glanced down at the horse beneath me. She'd been walking along so effortlessly that I'd almost forgotten I was riding her. "Do you have a guess as to who might be responsible for all these gifts?"

Carolyn didn't answer, but she did look thoughtful. Eventually, she spoke. "Are you sure you want to ruin everyone's fun by outing Santa?"

"Actually, I don't, but it is the job I've been assigned by my boss, and I really like my job. A job that I've barely begun. This is a good opportunity to show everyone that I have what it takes to be a good reporter."

Carolyn didn't answer at first. She seemed to be thinking things over as the horses slowly plodded along. Eventually, she spoke. "It seems to me that one of the most important attributes a reporter can possess is the ability to know the difference between reporting the news and manipulating the news."

I frowned. "I don't understand."

"Right now, there is an individual out there who is going around town gifting the town's residents with exactly what they need. Writing a story about this mystery Santa, and the good he is doing would fall under the category of reporting the news. But what do you think will happen if you out the guy or he or she finds out that you are planning to reveal Secret Santa's identity?"

"I suppose that you are thinking he or she might stop delivering the Secret Santa gifts."

"He or she might. And if he or she does stop delivering the gifts as a direct result of your article, you will have gone from reporting the news to manipulating the news."

I took a moment to consider this. I supposed Carolyn had a point. If I did reveal Secret Santa's identity and he stopped delivering his gifts, I supposed I'd have a different sort of story to write about, but it would be a story that came about because of my actions, so it would be one for which I was responsible. Angering Secret Santa was the last thing I wanted to do. Actually, angering the entire community was the last thing I wanted to do, but angering Secret Santa came in a close second. The question was, how was I going to keep both Secret Santa's secret *and* my job?

# Chapter 12

## Tuesday

I wasn't sure if it was my discussion with Carolyn the previous day or just my tendency toward insomnia that had me sitting in the attic window at two a.m. with only Alastair to keep me company, but I found that even the beauty of fresh snow on the frozen lake couldn't quite still the racing of my thoughts. Just twenty-four hours ago, I'd thought that being a real reporter and obtaining a staff position for the local newspaper was exactly where I wanted to take my life, but now I was less certain. I could see that being a reporter would be a job riddled with tough decisions at times. Decisions that would challenge me to take a hard look at my beliefs and my priorities. In this case, I found myself forced to decide whether it was more important to be a dependable employee who did my job and turned in my assignments as promised, or to listen to my conscience and allow Secret Santa to retain his anonymity.

"I really don't want to let Dex down," I said aloud to the cat. "He's been so good to me, and he has really taken a chance by letting me run with this story. I promised him I could do it, and I know I should."

"Meow."

I stroked the cat's head. "You do have a point. All I need to do this week is to write an article featuring the Secret Santa prospects. I don't need to make a final decision about a big reveal. Maybe I should just focus on that and hope everything works itself out by the time I am faced with the third article."

The cat began to purr loudly.

"Maybe once I interview Secret Santa, he or she will make it clear that they wouldn't really mind me revealing their secret. I know I've been clinging to this singular thought, and I know I've brought it up quite a few times, but finding that Secret Santa is after some publicity, after all, is the only way I am getting out of this unscathed."

I leaned back against the window frame behind me and slowly let out a breath. Tying myself up in a bundle of nerves was not going to accomplish anything. I needed to relax and clear my mind, so I focused on the warm and cheerful room and let my mind wander.

I'd plugged the tree and window lights in when I'd come up to the attic but had left the overhead light off. There was something magical about sitting in a dark room, with only tiny white lights to illuminate the space. I knew if there was anywhere that would allow my mind to settle, it would be up here in the attic, where I'd always found solace.

As I watched the snow falling gently outside the window, I thought about my mission to unmask, or in this case, unbeard Secret Santa. Yes, I had a decision to make, but I supposed the reality was that decision would be mute if I failed to figure out who the mysterious gift giver was. Carolyn had been a good lead, but after speaking to her, I was fairly certain it wasn't her running around granting wishes behind the veil of anonymity. Randy from the bank hadn't been any help, and when I'd spoken to him yesterday afternoon, Smitty from the snow removal service swore the gift card for Gilda Fredrickson had been purchased anonymously. I supposed I could still track down whoever handled the sale of Stephanie Baldwin's oven, although she had told me she'd tried to find out who'd sent it to her and was told the gift giver did not wish to be identified.

I'd spoken to all the Secret Santa gift recipients except Donnie Dingman, who'd been gifted with a used four-wheel-drive vehicle. I supposed I'd track him down today and see what he might know and be willing to tell me. Now that Carolyn had been eliminated from the suspect list, I supposed the most likely Secret Santas were Dean and Martin Simpson. I'd ask Cass to try to arrange a meeting between the tech billionaires and myself when I saw him this afternoon.

"Should we try to go back to sleep?" I asked the cat, who replied with a yawn.

I pulled him into my arms and stood up. I clicked off the white lights as I left the attic and headed toward the stairs. I supposed that life was riddled with difficult choices, and all I could do, all any of us could do, was to make the best choice we could at the time we were required to make it. I really didn't know what I was going to do about Secret Santa, but I couldn't do anything in the middle of the night, so I'd put the decision aside and try to get at least a few more hours of shuteye.

I thought about other decisions I'd made in my life. The decision to leave Foxtail Lake in the first place. The decision to skip college and set aside the other aspects of my life to focus on my music. The decision to leave the life I'd built in New York and return to Foxtail Lake after the accident. The decision to pursue a career in journalism after a random article about the death of my childhood friend sent me down that path. I liked to think of myself as being a purposeful sort who acted with intention, but as I thought about my life choices, I realized that I was a lot more likely to make a choice on a whim rather than devoting much time to gathering data and then making an informed decision. When I'd decided to devote my life to music, I certainly never took the time to research careers in music, and then decide if that was the right choice for me. I'd simply followed my heart and arranged my life accordingly.

Of course, if I were honest, music was more of a passion than a whim. I played because I found comfort in my music during a time in my life when nothing made sense and everything felt out of place. Could writing serve the same purpose in my life? Was a career in journalism my destiny, or was it yet another whim created by an opportunity presented at just the right time?

# Chapter 13

"Oh, I don't know," I said as I stared at my reflection in the mirror. When Hope had mentioned green tights and a red sweater, I was expecting something pretty bad, but this was downright horrifying.

"You look cute," she encouraged.

"I look ridiculous." The sweater adequately covered all my delicate spots, and it did fall to a point just past mid-thigh, but the green tights and red boots were just so… "Don't you think this costume is pretty stereotypical. I mean, if you really think about it, the real Santa lives in the North Pole. It's cold there. Even colder than here. I seriously doubt the elves are running around in such a skimpy uniform. No," I insisted, "they most likely wear heavy pants and waterproof boots."

Hope raised a brow. "The real Santa?"

I shrugged. "Hey, if I'm going to be an elf, I'm going to believe in the real Santa. Maybe I could find some green pants that would work just as well. Or at the very least, heavier leggings. I feel sort of naked. Actually, I feel totally naked. I can even feel a draft in a spot where I ought not to be feeling a draft."

Hope laughed. "If you want to wear heavier leggings and can find some in green, go for it. How do the boots fit?"

"They're a little big, but they're fine. It's not like I'm going to be walking anywhere in them."

"Great. So, I have you scheduled on Saturday morning and Sunday afternoon. The shifts are four hours. I'll email you an official schedule."

"And after the weekend?"

"I'm still working on a schedule, but I'll let you know if I need you."

"Okay. I guess I can make this work. I do want to help, but..." I waved a hand down the front of my body.

"Like I said. You look adorable. And we do expect to have a busy weekend, so I will need all the volunteers I can get. I really do appreciate this."

"I know, and it's fine. I'm sure I'll have fun with it, and I know how important this weekend is for the town."

"It is important, which is why I'm hoping the storm that is supposed to blow through here takes another path entirely. I hear they are predicting four feet of snow. That will close the pass for sure."

"Yeah," I agreed. "That is a lot in a short time. I remember the pass being closed for days at a time when I lived here before."

"It still is if we get enough snow or if whiteout conditions exist. Of course, this is Tuesday, and the event isn't until Saturday, so anything can happen. I guess all I can do is be prepared for whatever happens."

"That sounds like a good attitude to me." I set the red and green hat on my head just to get the full effect. I had to admit that it was not an effect I was thrilled with.

"So, how did your interview with Carolyn go?" Hope asked after I removed my hat and sat down to remove the boots.

"Except for the fact that she tried to kill me, it went fine."

She chuckled. "Kill you?"

"She wanted us to talk while she exercised her horse. Until yesterday, I'd managed to get through my entire life without mounting one of those beasts. To say I was terrified would be putting it mildly, but I survived."

"I've ridden with Carolyn. She has some pretty tame horses."

"She does. I rode a mare named Gaia. She was actually very sweet. Not that I'm looking to repeat the experience anytime soon, but I guess there is a part of me that is glad I faced my fear and didn't let it interfere with my goal of conducting the interview."

I picked up my street clothes and stepped behind the dressing screen.

"So do you think Carolyn is Secret Santa?"

"No," I answered after pulling my sweater over my head. "She made some good points about the fact that while she does frequently contribute to the community and often helps individuals out as well, she had never found the need to do so anonymously. That very point had occurred to me before, but after she said basically the same thing I'd already thought, I realized she wasn't the person I was looking for."

"Yeah, I had my doubts that it was her, but now you know for sure."

"I do. And that has value." I stepped out from behind the screen once I'd finished changing out of my elf costume.

"So, what is your plan now?" Hope asked.

"I have an appointment to interview Haviland Hargrove this afternoon. If it turns out he isn't Secret Santa, I am going to ask Cass to arrange a meeting with the Simpson brothers. Actually, I should speak to them either way. I am supposed to be doing an article about the suspects this week. I suppose I should include more than two."

"And if it isn't Haviland or Dean and Martin?" Hope asked.

I shrugged. "No idea. Others may have the means as well, but I can't think of anyone else off hand. I don't suppose you have any ideas?"

"Have you considered Mary Anderson? She is wealthy enough to be Secret Santa, and she is a very nice woman with a kind heart. I could totally see her wanting to help people out."

I paused. "Are you referring to Mrs. Anderson? My third grade teacher?"

"Yes. She is retired from teaching, of course."

"I don't remember her being particularly well off."

"She wasn't when you lived here before, but then she won the lottery."

My eyes widened. "You're kidding. Did she win a lot?"

"Several million dollars if I remember correctly. And unlike a lot of lottery winners who blow through all their money, she continued to live very conservatively. I can't say that I know her net worth, but I would guess that she could pull off the Secret Santa gifts if she wanted to."

I smiled. "Thanks. That sounds like a wonderful lead." I handed her the folded costume. "I would say I owe you, but after agreeing to the elf gig, I think I consider us even."

She laughed. "I agree. In fact, I think I still owe you, but I'm sure you'll find a way to collect."

# Chapter 14

When I arrived at the shelter for my training session that afternoon, I was introduced to Barkley. Barkley was a new arrival whose elderly owner had been forced to move into an assisted living facility after suffering a stroke. Barkley, I quickly found out, didn't need me to train him on basic commands, what he needed was for someone to coax him out of the depression he'd fallen into.

"Barkley is a unique situation," Naomi explained. "He is an older dog who has lived in a quiet home free of children and other animals for his entire life. The man who adopted him as a puppy was already well into his senior years when Barkley came to live with him, and given his reclusive nature, Barkley isn't used to interacting with anyone other than this one person."

"So now that his owner is no longer in his life, he is feeling lonely and depressed."

She nodded. "Exactly. And it will be close to impossible to find someone to adopt a dog who doesn't respond to the presence of people in any way. What I need you to do is to sit with him and talk to him. Simply spend time with him, so that he gets to know you. I'm hoping that after a while, he will start to respond to your presence. Once that happens, we can expose him to some of the other trainers. I don't think he'll ever be a super social dog, but I do hope we can get him to the point where he will at least look at those individuals who come to the shelter looking to adopt a senior dog."

"Okay," I agreed. "I'll see what I can do."

"Excellent. You have a peaceful way about you. I think that with some time, Barkley will begin to respond to your presence."

After Naomi left, I sat down on the floor next to Barkley. The entire time Naomi and I were chatting, he had simply laid on the floor with his head resting on his paws. He hadn't moved or responded in any way to our presence in the room. I supposed I didn't blame him. I'd be depressed too if the person I'd always depended on was suddenly stripped from my life.

"So my name is Callie," I said as a means of introduction. "I guess it is my job to coax you out of your depression, but I just want to say that I get it. I do. I've suffered crippling loss in my life as well, and I know how it is when everyone wants you to feel better before you are ready to even start dealing with your loss." My heart went out to the poor dog. "Grief is a real thing, and it takes as long to process as it takes. I just want you to know that you and I are cool. I'll sit here and chat with you, but there won't be any hard feelings if you need more time to really work through this loss."

I knew the dog was alive because he was breathing, but as far as I could tell, he hadn't moved an inch since I'd been introduced to him.

"So I'm dealing with an interesting situation of my own," I continued. I figured the dog wouldn't really care what I talked about, so I might as well use the time to process my own situation. "I am trying to work my way into a full-time job at the local newspaper, a job I never even knew I wanted until a few weeks ago, but want desperately now. Anyway, my boss, a really nice guy named Dex, has assigned me to do a series of articles about Secret Santa. The series is going to be reprinted in the Post, which is a huge opportunity for both me and the Foxtail News. Anyway, Dex wanted to put another reporter with more experience on the assignment, but the idea was mine in the first place, so I talked him into letting me run with it. The thing is, even though I promised the guy I would be able to meet all the requirements of the series, including naming Secret Santa, I am beginning to have doubts on so many levels. Not only am I beginning to doubt my ability to actually identify this guy, but even if I can figure out who he or she is, I am conflicted about making the identity of Secret Santa public."

I took a breath and then continued. "I was just chatting with Aunt Gracie's cat about the situation this morning, and he seemed to think I needed to really dig down and decide where my priorities lie. To be honest, I've been going over that in my head all day. The thing is that I just don't know what I should feel, and I certainly can't figure out how I do feel. On the one hand, if I am able to identify Secret Santa, which is the task I have agreed to, I know I have a responsibility to Dex to write the story I promised him I could and would write, and I know he is depending on me. On the other hand, I do feel like the guy who has been doing all these amazing things has a right to his anonymity."

Barkley still hadn't moved or responded in any way, but my job was just to talk to him and get him used to me, so I continued.

"Of course, worrying about whether to reveal the identity of Secret Santa may be premature since I really have no idea who he or she is. Do you know I actually rode a horse for the first time in my life just to get an interview with Carolyn Worthington? Now, if that isn't dedication to my article, I don't know what is. The horse was huge. I was sure I was going to fall and break my neck, but I didn't." I paused. "In fact, I actually had fun once I started to relax a bit. Not that I am looking to repeat the experience anytime soon, but I guess my fear of horses is one of those fears that was based on nothing more than the unknown."

I reached out slowly and put a hand on the dog's head. I gently ran my hand down his neck. He didn't respond, but I felt confident he was aware of my presence.

"Anyway, long story short, Carolyn told me she is not Secret Santa, and I believe her. So today, I went to visit a man named Haviland Hargrove. I guess he inherited a bunch of money, and he doesn't work. In fact, it seems like he really doesn't do much of anything. While he lives on a large estate in a gorgeous home, it seems like he lives a pretty lonely life. During our discussion, he didn't mention any friends or hobbies. Tom has mentioned him a time or two, so I guess the guy might go to the lodge occasionally. Still, living all alone in that big house seems pretty empty." I stroked the dog's head once again. "You know, Haviland might be a good fit for you. The guy lives alone, and I didn't see any other animals. It seems as if he is a low energy sort of guy, so he probably wouldn't make a lot of demands on you. I'll talk to Naomi about it."

I swore the dog lifted the very edge of his tail in a wave of approval, but I couldn't be sure. I'd seen stuffed dogs who seemed more animated.

"So anyway, after speaking to Haviland, I've decided he can't be Secret Santa," I continued. "He certainly has enough money, but Secret Santa has gone to a lot of effort to arrange for the gifts he has presented. I just don't see Haviland making that type of effort. Besides, Secret Santa knows exactly what his gift recipients need. That tells me he knows these people and is active in the community. Haviland most definitely is not."

I continued to run my fingers through the dog's soft fur as I spoke.

"At this point, the only real Secret Santa suspects I still need to speak to are the Simpson brothers and a woman named Mary Anderson, who just happens to have been my third grade teacher. If they don't turn out to be behind the gifts, I'm really not sure where to look next." I leaned back against the wall in an effort to support my back. Ever since my accident, I had a hard time sitting for long periods with my back not supported. "I guess I should talk to Cass about it when he gets here. He knows the brothers, so he should be able to arrange for me to talk with them. He might even have new updates on Secret Santa I haven't heard about yet. He is a cop, so sometimes he hears things before anyone else does. Of course, he's been pretty busy with his own case, so who knows if Secret Santa is even on his radar. And Hope might be able to help me get an interview with Mrs. Anderson."

"Callie," Cass called out.

I looked at the dog. "Speak of the devil." I sat forward and called out that I was in the training room.

"There you are," Cass said, poking his head in from the hallway. "Are you taking a break?"

"Actually, this is Barkley. He is a new dog who is dealing with depression. Naomi wanted me to sit and chat with him, so that's what I've been doing. Is Milo with you?"

"Milo is at the vet, getting his teeth cleaned. I need to pick him up when I am done here." Cass sat down on the other side of Barkley. "Hey, buddy. What's going on?"

The dog actually thumped his tail, although he still hadn't lifted his head.

"I'm afraid Barkley's owner had a stroke and had to go into assisted living. He couldn't bring Barkley along. The poor guy is feeling lost and out of sorts."

"Well, I guess so. Poor guy."

"Naomi mentioned that he is a quiet dog who is used to a quiet environment. Haviland Hargrove comes to mind as a human who might be a good match. I went and visited him today, and it seems like he is living all alone out there on that huge estate."

"Haviland would be a good choice," Cass agreed. "I'll talk to Naomi about it, and if she agrees, I'll approach him."

"So, the two of you are friends?"

He shrugged. "Sure. As much as Haviland is friends with anyone."

"He seems like the sort who prefers to keep to himself."

"Generally, that is true. He has a small circle of friends, but he isn't one to want to be social beyond that small circle." Cass scratched Barkley behind the ears. "Should we grab some dogs and take them into the playroom?"

"You go ahead. I'll meet you there. I think I'll sit with Barkley for a while longer."

"Okay." He stood up and started toward the door.

"Cass."

He paused and turned. "Yeah."

"I'm running into a dead end with my Secret Santa article. Do you think you could make an appointment for me to speak to Dean and Martin Simpson?"

"You still think they are Secret Santa?"

I shrugged. "Maybe. Even if they aren't, I really need to talk to them for this week's article about all the Secret Santa suspects."

"Yeah, okay. I'll call them. If they aren't busy, we can swing by their place this evening. They live out by the lake, so we'll just drop your car off on the way. After we drop off your car, we can stop at my place, so I can change and drop off Milo, and then we can meet with Dean and Martin. After that, we can go to dinner, and then I'll take you home when we're done."

"That sounds perfect. And thank you."

He winked at me and walked away. He sure was sexy in his uniform.

# Chapter 15

Dean and Martin were brothers who I estimated to be in their mid-forties. They lived together on a gated estate with a private lake. Several years ago, the brothers had sold a software company they'd started in their garage when they were in their teens for several billion dollars, after which they'd retired to the lake to tinker with their pet projects. I'd never met the men, but based on what I'd heard about them, they were both brilliant and introverted. Cass had told me that they had a small circle of friends they spent time with, but generally, they simply enjoyed each other's company.

I was grateful that Cass was included in the small circle of friends since I was fairly sure that I'd never have gotten past the front gate without him. Since the men didn't hang out in town often, it was equally unlikely that I would simply have run into them and convinced them to chat.

"Dean, Martin, this is my friend, Callie," Cass introduced after one of the brothers, I think Dean, had answered the door and invited us in.

"I'm so happy to finally meet you both," I said. "And I am grateful that you've agreed to take a few minutes to speak to me for my article."

"Anything for Cass," said the taller of the two brothers, who I was pretty sure was Dean.

"Let's head into the living room and talk by the fire," suggested the second brother, Martin I was pretty sure, who was blond and slightly shorter than his sibling was. "So how can we help you?"

"I guess you have heard about Secret Santa," I jumped right in after having a seat on the sofa in front of the fireplace.

"We have," Dean answered.

"I'm doing a story on the man or woman behind the anonymous gifts for the Foxtail News."

"And you think we are Secret Santa?" Martin asked.

"Are you? You certainly have the financial wherewithal to have purchased what I estimate is more than a hundred and fifty thousand dollars' worth of gifts so far if you count the new heating system I just found out Secret Santa had installed at the senior center and the new x-ray machine purchased for the clinic."

"That is substantial," Martin looked impressed. "But I'm afraid we can't take credit for these incredible gifts presented to the community, or for the gifts presented to individual residents of the community. Have you spoken to Carolyn Worthington?"

"I have, and it isn't her."

"It seems that an x-ray machine for the clinic is a pretty specific gift. Chances are that Doctor Nolan knows who is behind the gift. Maybe you should speak to him," Dean suggested.

I nodded. "Thank you. That is a good idea. I'll do that. Can you think of anyone else who might be Secret Santa, assuming that you are telling the truth, and it isn't the two of you?"

Dean raised a brow. "You think we would lie?"

"If keeping your secret was important enough, then yes, I think you might."

Martin laughed. "The woman just met us, and she already has us figured out." He looked at me. "And yes. If we were Secret Santa and we didn't want anyone to know, we would lie about it. But we aren't Secret Santa, so I'm going to suggest you move on."

"If it were me trying to identify Secret Santa, I think I would ask myself why now," Martin commented.

"What do you mean?" I asked, furrowing my brow.

"Everyone you have mentioned as a possible Secret Santa has lived in the area for a number of years, and everyone on your list has had the means to be Secret Santa for quite some time. If Secret Santa is someone who has lived in the area and had the means to buy gifts for members of the community for years and years, why now? Why not last year or the year before that?"

"So you think that Secret Santa might be someone new to the area?" I asked. It did seem that Martin had made a good point.

"Or someone who has recently come into wealth and felt moved to share it," Martin answered.

"What about Mary Anderson?" I asked. "I understand she won the lottery."

"She did," Cass jumped in. "But she won her money more than five years ago, and she has lived in Foxtail Lake for a lot longer than that."

"We found out that Buford Norris inherited a bunch of money," I said. "Of course, while the Secret Santa gifts began before he died, there have been a lot of gifts delivered since he passed, so I guess it can't be him. As far as you know, has anyone else in the community recently inherited a big chunk of money?"

"Justice Bodine," Dean and Martin said at the same time.

"Who is Justice Bodine?" I asked.

"Justice is the heir to the Bodine Lumber fortune," Cass said. "His family has been logging in the area for generations. Layton Bodine passed away over the summer, and Justice inherited everything." Cass paused. "Justice has the means to have purchased the gifts, but to me, he doesn't seem to have the right personality. In fact, I don't think he has even been home since he received his inheritance. At the biweekly poker game a few weeks ago, the guys were talking about the fact that he took off for Paris months ago and no one has seen him since."

"Yeah, I guess that's true," Dean admitted.

Martin shrugged. "Sorry that we couldn't be more help."

"It's fine. I really appreciate you taking the time to speak to me at all. Would you be willing to give me some personal information and maybe a few anecdotes for my column next week? It would really help me out."

Both men agreed to my request, so at least our trip out to their estate wasn't a total waste. Cass had told me from the beginning he didn't think the brothers were Secret Santa. I guess he was right, but if it wasn't them, I was getting pretty low on suspects. I still needed to contact Mary Anderson, which I would do tomorrow, but after Martin's comment about the timing of the whole thing, I was beginning to have my doubts on that front as well.

"Do you know which Secret Santa gift was the first?" I asked Cass as he drove toward the restaurant where we planned to have dinner.

"Actually, I'm not sure. I think it might have been Billy Prescott's wheelchair or perhaps the down payment on the diner. I suppose you can check with Billy's mother and with Connie and compare dates if it is important."

"I'm not sure it is important, but it might be. I can't get Martin's comment about why now out of my head. I wonder if Secret Santa didn't start with a specific gift for a specific purpose, and then once that gift was given, he caught the bug and kept going."

"I guess knowing the order which the gifts were given might be a good piece of information to have. You've spoken to most of the recipients. I'm sure if you give them a call, they will provide you with the dates you're after."

"I wonder if there have been any Secret Santa gifts that never made it to my list. The list I have has been created as folks have mentioned instances of gift giving to me, but I really have no way to know if I have them all. Is there anyone in town who would be the most apt to know all the local news? Maybe someone who enjoys gossip, and is in a position to know what is going on?"

"Nora Nottaway. She is usually in the know if something is going on."

Of course, Nora had been sick, so I wasn't sure she'd been spending as much time at the general store as she normally did, but I supposed it wouldn't hurt to stop by and say hi. The real challenge would be to act naturally in spite of what I knew. Keeping secrets, I knew from experience, wasn't always as easy as it might seem.

# Chapter 16

## Thursday

No one was more shocked than I was when Cass officially brought Ford Fisher in for questioning concerning Buford Norris's murder. We'd talked about the fact that Ford had been withdrawn since Buford's death, but Cass had seemed certain that Ford was not the killer he was looking for, assuming there even was a killer. Unfortunately, even the coroner couldn't say for certain what had caused the blow to Buford's head or even if the blow was the stimulus that caused him to pass out and freeze to death. The last I'd heard, it had been deemed equally likely that

Buford had died as the result of an accident as it was that he'd been murdered.

"I know I was the one to say that some of the guys at the lodge suspected that something was up with Ford due to his odd behavior, but I really never believed he would kill one of his best friends." Tom shook his head in disbelief as he, Aunt Gracie, and I discussed the situation over breakfast.

"So far, all I heard is that Cass brought him in for questioning," I pointed out. "That doesn't mean that he plans to arrest him. When I spoke to Cass about it before, he didn't think Ford was guilty."

"Maybe he found new evidence," Gracie said.

"Perhaps or maybe he just stumbled across some information he needed to follow up on," I countered.

"If it was as simple as that, why not just go to his house and chat with him?" Tom asked. "Why bring him into the station? That act alone makes him look guilty of something."

"That's true," I admitted. "I haven't spoken to Cass. I only know about the situation at all because I spoke to Hope, who'd found out from Rafe, that Ford had been brought in."

Rafe Conway was one of Cass's assistant deputies.

"I know that Cass planned to have a discussion with a man named Rupert Wooly yesterday. Maybe Rupert had new information that cast suspicion on Ford," I suggested.

"Rupert and Ford are friends of sorts," Tom acknowledged. "I suppose if Ford is somehow involved in whatever is going on with Buford, Rupert might know about it. Unlike a lot of the guys, who live in the area full-time, Rupert tends to be a drifter who moves in and out of town on a whim, but when he is in town, he does tend to hang out with the gang from the bar."

"Was he in town when Buford died?" I asked.

Tom nodded slowly. "I seem to recall he was. I think he left shortly after. I wasn't even aware he was back."

"Somehow, Cass knew," I informed the others. "He asked Naomi to track him down."

"Yup," Tom picked up his coffee mug. "That makes sense. For some reason unbeknownst to me, Rupert and Naomi are close. If anyone would know where to find the old coot, it would be her."

"Maybe you can stop in and talk to Cass later," Gracie suggested. "Find out what is going on. I have to admit to being curious."

"I'll stop by Cass's office after my appointment with Mary Anderson."

"Are you still trying to track down Secret Santa?" Tom asked.

I nodded. "Trying, but not having much success, I'm afraid. Honestly, Mary is my last Secret Santa suspect, and even I have to admit that she is a weak lead."

"And what if it turns out Mary is not Secret Santa?" Gracie asked.

I nibbled on my lower lip. "I do have one other idea. I guess you heard that the clinic got a new x-ray machine. Now, that is a costly gift. If Mary doesn't admit to being Secret Santa, I think I'm going to stop by and talk to Doctor Nolan. An x-ray machine isn't the sort of thing one just orders from an online catalog. I feel like Doctor Nolan had to have been in on the decision as to which machine to get."

"I agree," Gracie said. "It does seem that the machine is one gift the recipient would have to have been in on from the beginning."

I glanced at the clock. "I'd better head upstairs and get ready." I picked up my plate and utensils and stood up. "Do you need me to bring anything back from town?"

"If you wouldn't mind running by the market for potatoes, that would be wonderful," Gracie said.

I set my dishes in the sink. "I'd be happy to. How many do you need?"

"Just get ten pounds. I'm making chowder for dinner, but I'm sure I'll use the rest in the next couple of weeks with the holiday and all."

I went back to the table and gathered up my coffee mug and napkin. "Anything else?"

"No. That is all I can think of. Will you be home for dinner tonight?"

"I will. Paisley is coming over after school. I'll see if she wants to stay for chowder as well."

"I spoke to Ethel yesterday when I dropped Paisley off at home after her piano lesson. She mentioned that both she and Paisley are doing better. I guess they've settled into a routine that seems to work for both of them."

"That's wonderful," I grinned. "I will admit that I've been worried about the situation."

"Ethel thanked me for helping out. She said that Paisley really adores you, and she thinks that having you to talk to is really helping her through this difficult time."

I set my mug in the sink. "You know I'm happy to help out. Paisley is a great kid. I really enjoy spending time with her. In fact, in many ways, I feel like her being here and wanting piano lessons is what encouraged me to move on from my own loss. I guess I owe her quite a lot."

"I think the two of you were meant to help each other during this difficult time in both your lives."

I had to agree with that. It did my heart good that I'd been able to help Paisley, but I knew in my heart that she had helped me as well.

After I showered and dressed, I checked my phone for messages. Surprisingly, there was one from Martin Simpson letting me know that he had been able to confirm that Justice Bodine was still in Europe, so I shouldn't go to all the effort of trying to track him down. Aw, not only was it sweet of him to take the time to track Bodine down but to take the time to track me down as well.

There was also a message from Cass letting me know that he'd spoken to both Naomi and Haviland about Barkley and that Barkley was going to spend some time with Haviland to determine if the two were compatible. I thought about the seemingly lonely man and the even lonelier dog and prayed that it would work out for both of them.

As long as I was at it, I flipped over to my email app. Most of what I had was junk, but there was an email from a woman I'd known in New York, who wanted to speak to me about a job offer. There had been a time when I'd considered returning to New York and looking for a job, but I was happy here. I knew in my heart that Foxtail Lake was where I was destined to build a life. I hit return and let my friend know that, while I was honored she'd thought of me, I'd decided not to return to the East Coast.

After checking my mail, I tossed my phone on the bed and started getting ready for the day ahead of me. My first interview would be with Mrs. Anderson. After that, I hoped to chat with Cass and then... I really had no idea. If Mary didn't turn out to be Secret Santa, I supposed I'd need to widen my search parameters. I just wished I had a better idea of exactly how to do that.

# Chapter 17

 Mary Anderson lived a relatively normal life in spite of her success in the lottery. She lived in the same nice but modest house she'd lived in before she'd won millions of dollars, and other than the new SUV in the front drive, there was nothing about her home or her person to suggest she was a wealthy woman. I'd done some research and found out that since she'd won her millions, she hadn't done as many lottery winners did and made a bunch of impulse purchases, nor had she engaged in expensive travel or spa treatments. In my mind, this made her a good prospect for Secret Santa. If she hadn't spent her winnings on herself maybe, she'd spent the money, or at least part of it, on others.

"Thank you so much for agreeing to speak to me," I said after she ushered me into her home.

"I'm happy to help out if I can. I think the world of your aunt. She is always there to pitch in with a project or lend a helping hand to a neighbor in need."

"She is pretty great," I had to admit.

She motioned for me to take a seat. "So you mentioned on the phone that you are doing an article for the newspaper on Secret Santa."

I nodded. "That is correct. It is a series, actually. Last week, I wrote about some of the gift recipients, and this week, I am focusing on potential residents who might turn out to be the mysterious Secret Santa."

She grinned. "I will admit the Secret Santa idea has been great fun. The gifts and the mystery behind the gifts have been the talk of the town for weeks now. Honestly, I wish I would have thought of such a creative idea. I feel like Secret Santa has not only benefited those he has bestowed gifts upon, but his presence has been a blessing to the community as a whole."

"And what exactly do you mean by that?"

"Secret Santa has reminded us that there is still good and magic in the world, even if at times, things occur to make it seem otherwise."

I had to admit that was true. "The mood of the town as a whole does seem to have been lifted by the gifts."

"So am I to understand that your goal is to reveal the identity of Secret Santa?" Mary asked.

"That does seem to be the question of the day."

She puckered her lips. "Personally, I wouldn't. I think that the idea that Secret Santa could actually be anyone is part of the wonder of the whole thing. As I mentioned earlier, I wasn't the one to think of the idea, but as I also mentioned, there is a part of me who wishes I was. Secret Santa has created a sense of goodwill in the town that I feel has been missing for a while. I don't plan to steal Secret Santa's thunder by piggybacking on what he is doing, but I do plan to up my own giving this year."

"I guess the feeling of joy the man has spread is somewhat infectious."

"Personally, the Secret Santa gifts have reminded me of the innocence of childhood belief. The happy feelings associated with that belief make me want to reach out and hug everyone."

I had to chuckle at that. "Yes, I guess I understand that. And I do get what you are saying. I think the wonderful feeling created by doing something for others can be contagious. As you have, I've noticed an elevation in the mood of the community as a whole since the gifts began arriving."

"And therein lies the true magic of a selfless gift."

I leaned forward a bit. "Do you think that revealing Secret Santa's identity will destroy the atmosphere of goodwill that has been created by the gift giving?"

"I think it might."

Yeah, I was afraid of that. I really wanted a full-time job at the newspaper, but at what cost? I supposed this was something I needed to take a serious look at before I turned in my second article on Monday.

After I left Mary's, I realized I had some time to kill before my appointment with Donny Dingman, the only one of the original gift recipients I hadn't spoken to yet, so I decided to stop by the library and chat with Hope. Hope was a decade older than I was, but she was a person I'd connected with on an intimate level from the moment I'd met her as a teenager. I felt like we really understood each other. I considered us close friends and knew that I could talk to her about pretty much anything.

"So, what have you heard about Ford being taken in for questioning?" Hope asked the minute I walked in through the front door of the library.

"Nothing. I plan to go by and chat with Cass later, but I've been doing Secret Santa interviews this morning. Do you know if he was released or arrested after he was questioned?"

"I'm not sure. There has been a lot of gossip going around this morning, but no one seems to know anything for certain. I've texted both Cass and Rafe, but neither has texted me back. I know Ford has been acting oddly. Definitely out of character. But he wouldn't kill anyone, especially not Buford. The men had been friends for a long time."

"Yeah. Tom, Gracie, and I had the same discussion over breakfast."

Hope plopped her elbows on the counter in front of her. "I just don't understand this whole thing. Nothing has made a lick of sense since the minute I found out that Buford was dead. I'd talked to him that day... the day he died. He was happy and in a good mood. He'd been working on a project he was really excited about, and he mentioned his plan to head over to the bar for a drink to relax with the guys. Knowing Buford, I can see how it is possible he had one drink too many and ended up in a scuffle. I heard he fought with Dennis Felton, and if it turns out that he scuffled with Ford as well, I won't be surprised. Buford could be a mean drunk if he overdid it, but I absolutely cannot believe that anyone from Foxtail Lake would hit him over the head and leave him to freeze to death in a snowstorm. There has to be something else going on."

"Had you heard that Buford inherited a bunch of money a while back?"

Hope's gaze grew guarded. "Yes, I do know that. Do you think that his death is related to the money he inherited?"

"I think it might be. According to Cass, Buford cashed out and then hid the money. Cass has no idea what he did with it. He didn't appear to have made any investments, nor had he opened any bank accounts. There isn't evidence of large purchases or gifts to others. I did think that maybe Buford was Secret Santa for half a minute, but half the Secret Santa gifts have been delivered after his death, so it couldn't have been him. Besides, while I didn't know the man well, what I did know about him, doesn't lead me to believe he was the Secret Santa type."

"Maybe he hid the money in his home," Hope said.

"Cass looked. It isn't there. I think at this point, Cass is operating under the assumption that whoever killed him, took the money."

She frowned. "Oh, I don't know. I mean, who even knew about the inheritance at the time of Buford's death?"

"I don't think a lot of people did," I admitted, "but some of the guys from the bar knew." I glanced at the clock. "I gotta go. If you find out any more about

Ford, let me know, and if I find out anything, I'll text you."

"Sounds good."

# Chapter 18

Donnie Dingman didn't know any more about the person behind his Secret Santa gift than anyone else I'd spoken to, so I decided to take a chance and stop by the clinic. I wasn't confident that Doctor Nolan would know any more about the identity of Secret Santa than any of the other gift recipients did, but I figured that it couldn't hurt to stop by and speak to him about it.

"Sure, I know who purchased the x-ray machine."

"You do?" I really wasn't expecting that answer.

He nodded as his eyes danced with merriment. "Sure. The machine that was purchased is a very expensive and very specialized piece of equipment. I was the one who picked it out."

"So you know who Secret Santa is?"

He chuckled. "Yes, I guess I do."

"Who is it?" I held my breath as I waited for an answer.

"Secret Santa is a very good and giving individual who wishes to remain anonymous. I, for one, have no intention of spilling the beans, and if you want my opinion, you shouldn't either, even if you do manage to figure it out, which quite frankly, I don't think you will."

It seemed that keeping Secret Santa's identity a secret was a sentiment shared by pretty much everyone in town other than Dex.

"Look, I get that you are a reporter," Doctor Nolan continued. "And I get that it is a reporter's job to uncover and report the truth, even if that truth will hurt an exceptionally awesome person in the end. But this is a small town, where relationships matter. I don't think it is going to do you, or the newspaper any good to reveal a harmless secret no one really wants to be revealed."

"So it is your opinion that members of the community will be angry if Secret Santa's identity is revealed."

"And how. In my opinion, if you plan to continue to live here in Foxtail Lake beyond the holiday, you might want to reconsider your plan to ruin everyone's fun."

I groaned and leaned back against the counter. "Yeah. I've come to that conclusion as well. Of course, it will probably mean that I'll be fired from a job I don't even technically have yet."

Doctor Nolan put a hand on my shoulder. "Dex is not an unreasonable guy. I've known him for a long time, and while I can see him totally being seduced by the chance to be reprinted in the Post, I think that once he has a chance to really think about things, he'll come around to our way of thinking."

"You think?"

He nodded. "I do. I've read the material you've published so far. It's good. Really good. Dex knows that. He won't throw away a reporter with potential over a single act of consciousness."

"You know if I don't do the story, he'll just assign it to Brock."

"I suppose that's true, but between you and me, I don't think Brock has the creativity to figure the whole thing out."

Creativity to figure the whole thing out. That, I realized, was a clue in and of itself.

After I left the clinic, I headed over to the sheriff's office. I knew Cass would be busy, but I hoped I was catching him at a good time, and he'd have a few minutes to catch me up. I was sure now that word had gotten out that he'd brought Ford in for questioning, half the people in town would be curious about the rest of the story. I was equally certain that he wouldn't have time to return everyone's call, but Cass and I had a special relationship, and I hoped he'd speak to me.

"I spoke to Rupert yesterday," Cass began after he'd indicated I should take a seat in the chair across from his desk. "He told me that Buford and Ford had exchanged fisticuffs during the afternoon of the day Buford died."

"Fisticuffs?" I asked.

"His phrasing. Anyway, he told me that he had no idea what the men were arguing about, but at one point, they were really going at it. Eventually, some of the other men who were hanging around broke it up, and after a bit of discussion, they sent Buford home to sleep it off. According to Rupert, Ford left on foot shortly after Buford left on foot. As far as I can tell, Buford never made it home."

"So do you think Ford followed Buford and the men continued their sparring match, resulting in Buford passing out in the snow?"

"I believe that is a possibility, which is why I wanted to call Ford in and have an official record of my discussion with the man."

"And?"

"And at first he blurted out that he was indeed responsible for Buford's death. He had me in a panic for a minute since I really didn't want to have to arrest the guy for murder, but then he elaborated."

"What did he say?"

"He confirmed that he and Buford had a disagreement over a favor Buford had asked of him that he was having second thoughts about agreeing to do. He shared that both he and Buford had been drinking, and the argument escalated to the point where punches were exchanged. He'd been stressing over the fact that one of the blows he'd delivered might have been the one that led Buford to pass out. He swears that the man was alive and conscious when he left the bar, but he also said it occurred to him that Buford could have had a delayed reaction and that he, in fact, had been the one to kill his best friend."

"Wow. Poor Ford. No wonder he has been so depressed. I assume that you aren't convinced that Buford died after having a delayed response to one of the blows delivered by Ford."

"I hope not, but I'm not a doctor or a coroner. I guess I'll have to wait to see what the coroner comes back with. If it is possible that Buford passed out due to a blow delivered by Ford, things are going to get complicated. At this point, I am holding Ford until I can have a discussion with the sheriff and the DA."

"I wonder why Ford didn't come to you and explain what happened at the time of Buford's death."

"I suppose he was scared. It's understandable that he would be."

"Yeah, I guess. So what are you going to do now?"

"As I already mentioned, I need to have a discussion with the sheriff and the DA to see what they want to do. I also plan to continue to look into things. If the blow to the head led to Buford's death, I'm not sure any sort of blow delivered with Ford's fists could have done that much damage. In my mind, Buford could have come across someone else between the time he left the bar and the time he fell down unconscious in the snow."

"Someone who hit him with a heavy object which, caused him to pass out."

"Exactly."

"Buford must have been in a real mood to have fought with Dennis and Ford on the day of his death. I wonder what was going on. At the beginning of this investigation, you told me that while Buford had been drinking, he hadn't really been all that drunk. If it wasn't the alcohol that turned him violent, what did?"

"I don't know. I guess he might have just been having a bad day. It happens."

"I spoke to Hope earlier, and she told me that she had spoken to Buford before he went to the bar. She said he was in a good mood, and that all he planned to do was throw back a beer with his friends. Something must have happened that changed his mood after he left the library."

Cass narrowed his gaze. "I hadn't heard that Hope had spoken to Buford on the day he died. I guess I'll stop by the library and have a chat with her. Maybe she can fill in some of the blanks. I'd really like to figure this out before the DA decides to prosecute Ford for Buford's death because, in my mind, it seems likely that he will do just that."

# Chapter 19

## Saturday

This just couldn't get any worse.

I looked at myself in the mirror and groaned. "I thought I was going to be wearing a sweater with the tights."

"You were," Hope confirmed, "but one of the volunteers ripped the sweater last week, so we needed an alternative."

"Ripped the sweater? You only had one sweater?"

"No, we have several, but the others are all checked out to other volunteers. The sweater that was ripped is the one we'd set aside for you to use this weekend. I know this costume is a bit much, but it was all we had with such short notice. Personally, I think you look adorable."

Adorable? The heavy red sweater that had fallen to a point just past mid-thigh had been replaced with a green leotard topping the green tights. The outfit did include a short red skirt that barely covered my backside, but when combined with the red boots, I looked more like a holiday hooker than an elf.

"Are you sure there isn't another option?" I turned just a bit to confirm that my backside was actually covered. It was, but still.

"I'm afraid this is all I have. But you really needn't worry. You are completely covered from the neck down. The shorts and t-shirts you probably wore over the summer were much more revealing."

I supposed Hope had a point. It wasn't like there was skin showing, but the overall effect was just so... I really didn't want to dwell on it. If wearing this outfit was going to help Hope, I'd do it. She'd been nothing but nice to me since I'd been back.

"Okay, where do I go, and what do I do?"

Hope explained the routine and sent me on my way. Santa was a man named Dover Ledford. He'd worked at the local hardware store in town for a lot of years before retiring, and seemed to know pretty much everyone who stopped by to grab a photo with Santa and to share their wishes. The four-hour shift I'd agreed to, actually flew by. I would have considered it a complete success had Cass not stopped by during the last hour, making me feel self-conscience about my outfit all over again.

"Aren't you a cute elf," he chuckled.

I wanted to tell him to bite me, but instead, I just smiled. "Are you working today?" I'd noticed that he was wearing his uniform.

"Rafe, Trent, and I are volunteering our time to provide security over the weekend."

"That's nice. Any problems?"

"Not so far. Are you volunteering all day?"

"Just until two. After that, I thought I'd look around and maybe grab a bite to eat. How about you? Will you be here all day?"

"My shift goes until five when Trent takes over. If you're still in town, maybe we can meet up and grab some dinner."

I nodded. "I'd like that. Text when you're done, and we'll figure out where to meet." I glanced back at the line. "I should get back."

"Okay. Have fun, and I'll see you later."

"Wait," I said as he started to walk away. "What happened with Ford? Did you arrest him?"

"No, he has been released on his own recognizance. I'm not saying he is totally in the clear, but at this point, we don't have enough to charge him, and I really don't consider him a flight risk. Besides, I'm fairly confident that the coroner will determine that the blows suffered during the fight Ford and Buford engaged in were not the reason he passed out."

"So, with time, he should be cleared."

"I hope so. We'll talk more over dinner."

I nodded as he walked away.

The rest of the shift flew by, and I was actually looking forward to tomorrow's volunteer duty. After I changed back into my street clothes, I headed toward the community center where the craft displays had been set up. I thought it would be nice to buy a hand-crafted decoration of some sort for Ethel. Other than the tree Paisley and I had purchased and decorated, she really hadn't taken the time to set out any other items. Perhaps a centerpiece for her dining table or a wreath for her door. Nothing that she'd have to fuss with, but something she would see often and could enjoy. I knew that Tom and Gracie planned to bring Paisley by later in the day. I supposed I'd spend some time with them before meeting up with Cass for dinner.

"Oh, good. I'm glad I ran into you."

I looked up from the table centerpieces I'd been looking through. "Hi, Dex. How are you? Were you looking for me?"

He nodded. "I have a job for you if you are free for a couple of hours."

I narrowed my gaze. "What sort of job?"

"I need someone to cover the ice fishing competition out at Logan Pond. Brock was going to do it, but he got held up with some family issues."

"What do you mean by cover?" I asked, picturing the frozen landscape and below freezing temperatures that covering the event was going to entail.

"I just need someone to head out there, take some photos of the participants with their fish, and maybe get a few quotes to weave into a story."

Okay, that sounded doable. "Okay. Should I go now?"

He nodded. "The event should already be underway. You can turn the photos and story into me on Monday, along with your Secret Santa story. How are you doing on it?"

I forced a smile. "Great. Really, really great."

As I drove along the frozen highway toward Logan Pond, it occurred to me that this assignment might actually be a godsend. I planned to let Dex know on Monday that I'd decided I was unable to identify Secret Santa. Maybe having a second story to offer would soften the blow a bit. When I arrived at Logan Pond, I was expecting to find the entrants spread out across the surface of the frozen lake, but instead found everyone standing in one location. I wasn't an expert on ice fishing, but wasn't everyone supposed to have their own hole?

"What's going on?" I asked the man closest to where I was standing after joining the group.

He stepped aside. I took a step forward and gasped. "Is that?"

"Ford Fisher," the man confirmed as my eyes focused onto the frozen body just below the surface of a thin sheet of ice.

# Chapter 20

"Has anyone called Cass?" I asked as soon as I was able to gather my thoughts.

"He's on his way," someone in the crowd said.

"What happened? Did he fall in?" I asked.

"Don't know," the man standing closest to me answered. "He was there just below the surface when we all arrived."

"I thought this event had been going on for a while now." Surely, these men hadn't been standing around gawking at the body under the ice for the past couple of hours.

"Snowmobile races went long. We just got here a few minutes before you did."

I guess that explained why they'd just called Cass. I knew he'd been in town, so I figured he'd be here in the next ten or fifteen minutes. He made it in eight.

"What do you think happened?" I asked Cass as we waited for the fire department to arrive. The local station had men equipped and trained for ice rescues. I supposed that even though this was a retrieval and not a rescue, they were the best equipped to handle things.

"I have no idea. I dropped Ford off at his home yesterday morning after I'd received word that the DA was going to do some more research before deciding whether to file charges. He told me he planned to stay in this weekend. He said he had some things he needed to go over in his mind. At no point did he mention coming out here to the pond. I really can't imagine why he was here."

"Maybe he decided to do some ice fishing," I suggested. "It would have been nice and quiet out here yesterday. Just the sort of place one might go to get in touch with their emotions."

Cass looked around. "That could be what occurred, but if he was here to fish and simply fell in, where is his stuff?"

Good question.

"And look what he has on," Cass continued. "He is wearing a jacket, but not the heavy down sort one would wear if they were going to spend any time out in the elements."

I supposed that was true.

"If I had to guess, I imagine we are going to find that Ford died elsewhere and was dumped here. I guess the coroner will be able to tell us whether he drowned or not, but before we can know any of that, we need to get him out of the water and down to the morgue."

I turned around at the sound of sirens. "It sounds like the fire department is here."

The next couple of hours were filled with the sounds of men shouting as strategies were discussed, and equipment was positioned. I decided to wait in my car. I couldn't quite bring myself to leave before the retrieval had been completed, but I didn't want to get in the way. Besides, it was cold. Very, very cold. Watching the action from the toasty interior of my car made the most sense any way you looked at it.

"I guess I'm going to have to take a raincheck on our dinner," Cass said after he slipped into the passenger seat of my car once the body had been taken away.

"I know. It's fine. Maybe tomorrow?"

"Maybe. I'll need to see how this whole thing plays out. Are you volunteering at the Santa House tomorrow?"

I nodded. "In the afternoon, from two until six. I'll probably come to town early in case Hope needs help with anything else. If you want to find me, I'll have my phone, so you can call or text." I looked out toward the pond. "Do you think this was an accident, or do you think someone put Ford in the lake?"

He paused, pursing his lips. "I'm not sure at this point, but my gut is telling me that Ford didn't simply wander out into the middle of the forest and fall into a frozen pond. His vehicle isn't anywhere in sight, nor is his fishing gear, as we discussed before. And as we also discussed before, he isn't dressed for ice fishing. I think we are going to find that we have another murder on our hands."

"It sounds like you are even more certain that Buford's death was a murder."

He nodded. "If it turns out that Ford was killed elsewhere and dumped here as I suspect, then yes, I'm even more certain that Buford was murdered as well."

# Chapter 21

## Monday

By the time Monday rolled around, Ford's death had officially been ruled a homicide. With the new evidence relating to Ford's death, Cass was even more determined to prove that Buford had been murdered as well. He'd been working a lot of hours, so we never had gotten around to having dinner together, but I was hoping he'd have some time to talk later this afternoon. I had to admit that I was anxious to find out what he had discovered by this point.

But before I could meet with Cass, I needed to meet with Dex. I had the second story relating the

Secret Santa mystery to turn in, and I had an article on Ford's body being found in Logan Pond as well. Both articles had turned out even better than I hoped, so I was fairly confident he would be happy with them. I just hoped that his satisfaction with this week's articles would prevent him from firing me over my refusal to unmask Secret Santa.

I'd given the situation a lot of thought, and while I did admit to being conflicted, I knew that in the end, I had to follow my conscience. I wanted a shot at being a real reporter, and I knew that at times real reporters followed the truth no matter who might end up getting hurt in the process, but I also knew there were reporters out there who followed their heart and their conscience first and foremost and that, I'd decided was the sort of reporter I wanted to be.

"Waffles?" Aunt Gracie asked after I emerged from my room dressed and ready to tackle the day.

"Just coffee."

"I have blackberry compote and whipped cream."

I did love blackberry topping. "Okay. Maybe just one."

Gracie handed me a mug of coffee. "So, what are your plans today?"

I took a sip of the coffee and then sat down at the empty table. "I have to meet with Dex, and then I'm hoping to meet with Cass and get an update on Ford Fisher's situation. Where is Tom this morning?"

"He's having breakfast in town with some of the guys from the lodge. I guess everyone is pretty freaked out about losing two of their own. They wanted to get together and discuss the situation."

"The whole thing is really odd. First, Buford dies under suspicious circumstances, and then Ford is found dead just a day after being released as a suspect in Buford's death. I don't know what is going on, but I would be willing to bet that the two deaths are related."

Gracie slid my plate in front of me. Boy, did it look good. In my opinion, having waffles with fruit topping and whipped cream for breakfast was a bit like having pie. Totally decadent and generally much enjoyed.

"Was Cass able to determine Ford's cause of death?" Gracie asked.

"He, like Buford, was hit over the head with a heavy object, only the injury to Ford was a lot more extensive. Cass said that he most likely died from the blow, whereas the cause of death for Buford seems to have been hypothermia. I'm not sure why the killer went to all the trouble to dump Ford's body in the lake. The fact that he did seems important to me. It appeared that Buford was hit and then left where he fell, but Ford was moved and then placed under the ice. That would require someone to make a hole in the ice so the body could be inserted. I have to wonder why someone went to all that trouble."

"It took a lot of effort," Gracie agreed. "Do you think there is symbolism at play?"

I frowned. "Like what?"

"I'm not sure exactly, but I do agree that even if the person who killed Ford didn't want to leave the body at the location of the murder for some reason, there are easier ways to dispose of remains. Even if he wanted to leave Ford at Logan Pond, why not just dump him on the shore or in the forest? Why go to all the trouble to chop a hole in the ice and slide the body into the water?"

I took a sip of my coffee. "I guess that is the question of the day. I know Cass has been struggling with it. Maybe he knows something by now."

"Maybe. I hope he figures this out soon. Tom and the other guys from the lodge are really worried about things. I think they are concerned that the reason Buford and Ford were targeted was because of their association with the lodge, and perhaps that could mean that one of them is next."

I paused to consider this. "I don't think the lodge is the common link. Ford and Buford were both at the bar on the day Buford died. I would think if there was a place that served as a common denominator, it would be the bar and not the lodge. But even that seems like a longshot. I suppose that being taken in for questioning in Buford's death could have led to Ford's death. I know Cass has considered that scenario."

"Why would Ford be killed for being questioned in Buford's murder?"

I shrugged. "Maybe whoever killed Buford suspected or even knew that Ford knew something that could help Cass to identify him or her, so the person who killed Buford decided to kill Ford before he could talk. Maybe the pond was chosen as the dump spot because it is shocking and public. The killer might even have known about the ice fishing competition."

"So the killer was trying to send a message."

"Perhaps."

"To who?"

I shrugged. "Maybe there is someone else out there who knows something the killer doesn't want to be told."

"Well, that's frightening."

"Yes," I agreed. "It is."

"Let's just hope that Cass can figure out who did this terrible thing and lock them up before they can hurt anyone else."

I licked the last of the whipped cream from my fork. "Cass is a good cop. He'll figure it out."

# Chapter 22

I had to admit that I was more than slightly nervous about my meeting with Dex. I wasn't sure if he'd be angry or disappointed in me or if he'd understand my trepidation and simply pass the story to Brock. I really wanted Dex to like me, and I really wanted to expand my hours at the newspaper, but I'd given the situation a lot of thought, and as I'd told Gracie, I really needed to follow my heart and my conscience.

"Hey, Gabby," I greeted the friendly receptionist after entering the building. "Is Dex here? I have my articles."

"Actually, he isn't here. I'm not sure if you heard, but there was a house fire on the north end of town this morning. Brock is still on leave due to issues of a personal nature, so Dex is covering it himself."

I frowned. "Was anyone hurt?"

"No. Based on what I heard, the Christmas tree caught fire after the lights were left on all night. I guess the tree is in a separate living area in a finished basement, and no one even knew it had been left on. The light sets used on the tree were old, and it looks like one of the strings may have shorted out. The kids had already gone to school by the time the fire started, and both parents were at work. There were a couple of cats indoors, but a neighbor got them out in plenty of time, so everyone is fine."

"I'm glad to hear that. I feel bad that the family lost their home, but homes can be replaced while people and pets cannot."

Gabby smiled gently. "I couldn't agree more. If the fire had started while everyone was sleeping, who knows what would have happened."

I pulled up a chair and sat down. "I know this is none of my business, but what's going on with Brock. When I saw Dex on Saturday, he mentioned that Brock was taking care of some personal issues, but I wasn't aware there was anything so serious going on that he would still be out this week."

"His wife left him. I don't think that is common knowledge at this point, so please don't say anything to anyone. Apparently, the couple had a huge fight on Friday, and she packed her bags and took herself and the kids to Virginia, where her sister lives."

"Oh, no. I'm so sorry to hear that. I've only spoken to Brock twice and even then only briefly, and I've never met his wife, but I hate to hear about families in crisis."

Gabby picked up her stapler and secured the stack of papers she'd been shuffling around since I'd been there. "According to Dex, Brock has asked to be off until after New Year's. He decided to go to Virginia to try to work things out. It is going to make things tough on Dex, but at least he'd decided to assign the Secret Santa story to you and not Brock. It would have been a real mess if he'd been the one responsible for the series."

"Yeah," I groaned. "A real mess."

Now, what was I going to do? I'd been all set to pass Secret Santa off to Brock, but now that wasn't going to work out. Maybe Dex would want to do the final story himself. Not that he had time to research Secret Santa now that he'd lost his only full-time reporter. The poor guy was going to have his hands full shuffling everything he was already doing with everything Brock had been assigned.

"I guess I'll just leave the photos and stories I have with you." I handed Gabby the envelope with the hard copy, photos, and thumb drive with digital copies of everything. "If Dex has any questions, he can call me. I know he is probably going to be swamped today, but I do need to talk to him. I guess maybe just pass that message along. My schedule is pretty flexible, so we can meet whenever it is convenient for him."

Gabby took the envelope. "Okay. I'll tell him."

"And let him know if he wants me to help pick up some of the slack, I can make myself available to cover other stories. I'm not sure what Brock was working on, but I'm sure Dex is going to have his hands full."

"I'm sure Dex will appreciate the offer, and I suspect he'll take you up on it. Not that there is ever a good time for Brock to be gone, but now with everything that is going on, it seems like a worse time than normal."

"Well, I'm willing to do what I can."

She smiled. "Dex really likes you, you know. I can tell. There have been other folks from time to time who've contributed stories on one event or another. Sometimes Dex runs them, but that is usually the end of it. After your first one, the one about the murder of those young girls, I could see that Dex was sold. I overheard him telling someone on the phone that you had real talent. A talent he hoped to hone and utilize in the future."

I grinned. "Thanks for telling me that. It means a lot."

"I think Dex was really impressed when you made your case about being assigned the Secret Santa series as well. Most people who basically have zero experience doing a series like that wouldn't have wanted to put themselves out there the way you did. Most wouldn't have been willing to take the risk. But you just jumped right in and went for it. I know that impressed Dex. Heck, it impressed me. I'm pretty sure if you are interested, you have a real future here."

I forced myself to continue smiling when all I wanted to do was cry. "I am interested in a future with the newspaper, and I appreciate everything you've said." I stood up. "I should go. Tell Dex to call me when he is ready to chat."

"I will, and good luck with the third installment of your series. I can't wait to see who Secret Santa is."

"Yeah, me too," I mumbled under my breath.

# Chapter 23

Cass was in his office when I stopped by. I immediately noticed the colorfully decorated tree on the corner of his desk. It was one of those live trees they sold at the market. I wasn't certain if he'd brought it in himself or if someone from the community had brought it by, but it did make the place feel a bit festive.

"So, how did your talk with Dex go?" Cass asked shortly after I'd taken a seat. We'd talked about the chat I'd planned to have with Dex, and he knew how nervous I'd been about it.

"It didn't go. I guess Brock has taken a leave from the newspaper until after New Year's, and Dex had to cover a house fire, so he wasn't in when I stopped by to drop off my stories."

Cass frowned. "I haven't heard about a house fire."

"The house that burned down is outside of town. I suppose the main dispatch might have sent someone from the Rivers Bend office. It might even be closer to where the fire occurred."

"Was anyone hurt?"

"Gabby says no. Which is good. It is too bad the family who lived in the house lost their home, but at least no one was home when the fire broke out. While devastating, it could have been worse."

He nodded. "Yes, it could have been. So what's going on with Brock?"

"Family stuff. It sounds like he is working on it, which is good, but I'm afraid that leaves me in a bit of a pickle. We talked about the fact that I'd decided that I didn't want to identify Secret Santa even if I do manage to figure out who he or she is, which at this point, isn't a given, so I'd planned to pass the story along to Brock, but now that he's out on leave…"

"There is no one to pass the story to."

"Exactly. I suppose that's Dex's problem, and he could do it himself if need be, but I can't do that to him. I'd feel like I was bailing on a sinking ship. I still don't want to do the story for all the same reasons I didn't want to do it the last time we spoke, but I also don't want to add to the pressure Dex must be feeling by telling him that I decided not to write the story I promised I would write and he is depending on me to provide."

Cass leaned back in his chair. He rocked gently front to back. "You are in a tough situation," he admitted. "Maybe you can convince Dex that it is a bad idea to reveal Secret Santa's identity. If you can, then you can write a lovely Christmas Eve piece minus the big reveal."

"That would be ideal, but with the Post in the mix, I doubt he will go for it."

"Yeah," he said, blowing out a breath.

"I let Gabby know that I was free to take on some additional assignments if Dex needed my help. I'm hoping that if I can help him fill the void left by Brock's absence, he won't fire me when he realizes that I was unable to finish my assignment."

"Perhaps, but it seems that unable to finish might be easier to stomach than unwilling to finish. If you are able to identify Secret Santa, but then refuse to give him up, I have a feeling Dex might take that personally. If you do your best, but simply can't figure it out, I'm not really sure how he can fire you over that."

"So, I should just continue to look for Secret Santa, but maybe not too hard?"

He shrugged.

"Don't you think he'll see through that? Maybe I should just be honest and take whatever consequences might come my way as a result."

"I suppose that might be the best way to deal with things, but I wouldn't wait. He might not be able to give the story to Brock as you hoped, but if you wait to tell him that you are unwilling to deliver the story he wants until it is too late, it seems to me that he'll be twice as mad."

"I know you're right. I'll let him know what is on my mind when we have our meeting. Maybe I will be able to convince him that not unmasking the guy really is the best thing to do for everyone involved."

"That's the spirit. A positive frame of mind wins out every time."

"I guess," I said, lifting a shoulder. "So, how are you doing with your cases?"

"Not as well as I'd like. We know Ford was definitely murdered. As I mentioned earlier, the trauma to his head is a lot more evident than the trauma to Buford's head. Still, I suspect the same person is behind both deaths. It looks as if Buford might have been hit where he fell. The blow to Buford's head didn't bleed, so it is hard to know for certain. Ford's wound, however, bled quite a lot. We found blood in his living room, so we assume he was killed in his home and then transported to the lake."

"So was there other evidence?"

"CSU is going over everything. They are looking for fingerprints and other physical evidence. The thing is that Ford has never been a good housekeeper, and things have been really bad since Buford died. The crime scene guys are never going to be able to pick out evidence such as clothing fibers in all the mess."

"That's too bad. Any clue at all as to who might have killed him?"

He slowly shook his head. "I suppose that the killer must be someone known to both Buford and Ford. Given the fact that Buford froze to death as a result of passing out, which could have been caused by the blow to the head, it does seem possible that the whole thing was just a terrible accident. If that is true, then the killer might even have confided in someone."

"Like Ford."

"Exactly. But then once Ford was brought in on the secret, the killer started having doubts about

Ford's ability to keep his secret, and once he was brought in for questioning, he panicked, so he killed him to keep him quiet."

"That explanation works for me, but how are you going to prove it?"

"I'm not sure. Yet. But I do plan to continue to work on it until I catch a break. It'll happen. It always does. Eventually."

"Have you spoken to any of the men's mutual friends? Maybe Ford wasn't the only one who knew what happened to Buford, assuming that is even what is going on, which at this point is pretty much nothing more than a shot in the dark, I suppose."

"I've interviewed everyone who is a member of the lodge both men belonged to as well as everyone who hung out at the bar they frequented. I've found that there are a lot of theories as to what is going on and who might be involved, but so far, I haven't found a consensus of any sort. Ford ended up in a frozen lake, so if there was ever any physical evidence on his body, it is most likely long gone, but I do have people looking for anything that will better define what happened."

"He must have been transported to the lake, assumedly in the trunk of someone's car or in the bed of a truck. I guess you can check out everyone's vehicle and look for blood."

"Actually, Rafe is already doing that. So far, every vehicle he has checked is clean, but not too clean, if you know what I mean."

"I do. If the vehicle had recently been scrubbed top to bottom, that would be suspect. What if the killer wrapped him in a blanket or a rug before transporting him? I suppose there might be something like that to find."

Cass nodded. "Perhaps, but unless someone left a bloody rug out with the weekly garbage, I doubt we'll find it without a search warrant. The same with the clothes the killer was wearing. They must have gotten blood on them."

I got up and began pacing around the room. I paced at times when I had something heavy on my mind, and the death of two men in the community was heavy indeed. "Rupert seemed to have been a witness to the altercation between Ford and Buford. Maybe he knows more than he said."

"I tried to talk to him again after Ford's body was found, but he's flown the coop. He does that. Fairly often, in fact. I called and spoke to Naomi, and she said she would keep an eye out for him. If he shows up, she'll call me."

"Do you think he had anything to do with Ford's death? The fact that he disappeared right after his body was found seems suspect."

He shook his head. "Not really. Like I said, it is Rupert's way to come and go. If I really had to guess..." Cass's cell buzzed. He looked down at the number displayed. "It's Rafe. I need to get it."

I nodded.

"Hey, what's up?" he asked.

I watched as his eyes grew wide. "How much did you say?"

He whistled. "Okay. I'll be right over."

He hung up and looked at me. "That was Rafe. I think I know who was behind the Secret Santa money."

My eyes grew wide. "Who?"

"Buford."

"Buford," I narrowed my gaze. "But at least half the gifts have been delivered since he died."

"I know. There is a bit of a story to it. I need to go, but if you want to ride along with me, I'll explain along the way."

I stood up. "Okay. I'm game. I can't wait to hear how is it that a dead man has been playing Secret Santa long after he died."

As it turned out, after Ford's body was found, Cass had been provided with a tip that it was possible that Ford might have a large amount of money hidden in his house. Cass had sent Rafe to check it out, and even though the crime scene guys had already been through the house, Rafe noticed a wall at the back of a closet that looked to have been painted recently. It wasn't really obvious that the paint was fresher than the rest of the paint in the home, and it was the same color, but it did look to be slightly brighter. On a hunch, Rafe took a sledgehammer to the wall and found more than fifty thousand dollars hidden inside.

"Wait," I said after Cass explained all of this to me. "If Buford was providing the money used for the Secret Santa gifts, why was the money in Ford's closet?"

"My source suspects that after Buford was gifted the money from his sister, he decided to simply cash it in and get rid of it. My source isn't sure why he would do that, but that is the theory. My source believes that, for some reason, Buford might not have wanted the money, but perhaps he didn't want his nephew to have it either, so he came up with the idea to give it away. Assuming that Buford knew the nephew would be looking for the money, he might have decided to liquidate and then hide it at Ford's place."

"So Ford continued to play Secret Santa even after Buford died."

"According to my source, Buford simply provided the money to someone else in the community who had the relationships and knowhow to select the recipients and arrange for the gifts. My source also said that they believe that the money was kept at Ford's place until it could be distributed."

I raised a brow. "Who is this source you keep talking about?"

"I'm afraid I can't tell you that."

I held my hands out in front of me. "Okay, wait. Let me make sure I have this straight. Buford is gifted a fortune from a sister he hadn't spoken to in forty years. We don't know why the siblings hadn't spoken or why the sister left the money to Buford in the first place, but that seems to be what happened."

"Yes. That is correct."

I continued. "For reasons we also don't understand, Buford didn't want the money, so he decided to give it away. He enlisted the help of someone in the community with connections who would identify the Secret Santa recipients and make the arrangements for the gifts to be delivered."

"Yes, that seems to be what happened."

"So selecting recipients and delivering gifts would take some time, but Buford must have known that the nephew would come looking for the money, so he liquidated and hid the cash at Ford's house. The money was distributed by Buford to the person in the community who was selecting the gift recipients for use in the Secret Santa campaign until he died, and then Ford continued to dole out the money in his stead."

"Sounds like you understand what we believe has occurred."

"And what is left of the money was still in Ford's wall?"

"It seems so."

I took a minute to let this sink in. "Okay, so if Buford trusted Ford enough to let him hang onto his money while it was being spent, why did the men fight on the day Buford died?"

"I don't know."

I bit down gently on my lower lip. "I do remember hearing that Ford and Buford had disagreed about something having to do with a favor Buford had asked of Ford. Maybe Ford no longer wanted to hold the money. Maybe the nephew had come around looking for it, and Ford felt that having it put him in danger."

Cass gently bobbed his head. "I suppose that could very well be. The problem is that the only two who would know for certain if that occurred are Ford and Buford, and both are dead."

Cass had a point. This was a theory that could never really be proven. "We know that both men had been drinking, so I suppose that a simple squabble could have escalated into something more." I looked at Cass as he pulled off the highway onto the mountain road where Ford had lived. "So, what does this mean? Does knowing that Ford had all that money help us to know who killed him?"

"No, not for certain, but it does seem to me that the money might have been the motive behind the deaths of both men, and if that is the case, my money is either on the nephew or someone from the bar that the men confided in who decided he wanted his cut of Buford's windfall."

# Chapter 24

## Tuesday

The snow gently drifted on air currents toward the ground outside the attic window. As I did on most nights when I couldn't sleep, I'd curled myself up inside the window with Alastair and a heavy blanket, and tried to focus on the beauty outside the window rather than the warring thoughts in my mind. The story Cass had come up with as to how the money had ended up in Ford's wall was a good one. He refused to tell me who tipped him off to the possible existence of the money at Ford's house, and who had been helping Buford and Ford with the Secret Santa gifts, but I'd given the matter a lot of thought and had come to my own conclusions. The question was what to do with that knowledge. I still hadn't had the opportunity to speak to Dex. He'd been super busy yesterday, as had I. He did send along an email letting me know he loved the articles I'd turned in, and was looking forward to the third article in the series next week. He'd also asked me if I'd be willing to take on some extra assignments while Brock was out. I'd answered that I would be delighted to take on any extra work he might have, but for reasons unbeknownst even to me, I never did bring up my hesitation with the Secret Santa story.

The more I thought about things, the more certain I was that I had the information I needed to pen the big reveal, but I still wasn't sure I wanted to follow through with the story. In fact, the more I thought about it, the less certain I was that revealing the identity of the person who'd arranged for the gifts was the right thing to do. I knew I needed to make a decision sooner rather than later, which probably accounted for my state of insomnia.

"I could simply reveal that Buford was behind the Secret Santa gifts without naming his helper," I said to Alastair.

"Meow."

"Yes, it has occurred to me that Dex will want more, and yes, I suppose that without confirmation from the helper, I don't even have proof that it has been Buford's inheritance that has been used to purchase the gifts. It does make sense, however. I'm not sure who Cass's source is, but it seems that it is someone who knows what they are talking about." I paused to roll the situation around in my head. "I'm not sure why this source didn't come forward after

Buford died if they knew what was going on. Of course, I suppose the source might not have realized that the money was the most likely motive for Buford's death until after Ford died as well."

I pulled the cat to my chest and leaned back against the wall behind me. The lights in the trees illuminated the exterior of the yard enough to see the new snow as it fell to the ground. It really was lovely. So pretty and serene. I wished I could still my mind enough to really enjoy it.

"Cass is working on a warrant to bring Buford's nephew in for questioning. He tried to speak to him over the phone after the money was found yesterday, but the man refused to cooperate. Cass thinks that the nephew who I seem to remember is named Jason, came to Foxtail Lake on the day Buford died to confront him about the missing money. Cass is assuming the men argued, which led to a physical altercation, which led to the head injury, which resulted in Buford passing out in the snow."

"Meow."

"Yes, Cass does have a solid theory," I agreed with the cat. "He also thinks that after Jason couldn't find the money, he left town, but when he heard about the Secret Santa gifts, he might have realized what must have happened to the money. Neither Cass nor I are sure how Jason knew about Ford's involvement in the whole thing. The two men were good friends, so I suppose he might just have put two and two together. We are assuming Jason confronted Ford about the money, Ford refused to tell him where what remained was hidden, and this resulted in yet another altercation, leading to another death."

Alastair wiggled out of my arms and jumped to the floor. I continued to speak, since talking to the cat really did help me to work things out in my mind.

"Yes, Cass will need to prove all of this, and no, as far as I know, he doesn't have any physical evidence to back up his theory." I crossed my legs under my body and leaned forward just a bit. "If the nephew was in town when Buford died and when Ford died, someone may have seen something. I imagine Cass has been asking around."

I uncurled my legs and slipped around, so my back was to the window, and I was facing the attic room. I'd turned on the white lights I'd hung everywhere, which gave the room a fairytale feel. The room was open and airy since Paisley and I had cleaned it. I'd set up a desk near the window where I liked to sit so I could work and look out at the lake. The old piano was on the wall closest to the door, and stacks and stacks of boxes were labeled and stored near the far wall. The boxes that had held the Christmas decorations had been pulled out and set to the side. Gracie had gone through them and removed the decorations she wanted to use this year. There were still a few items in the boxes, but overall, it seemed as if almost everything had found a place to be displayed.

There were a few items too large for boxes, such as an old artificial tree, a life-size plastic Santa that used to be in the yard, a candy cane fence that at one time lined the walk, and a walking cane disguised as a candy cane. I remembered that Gracie had used the cane in a play she'd participated in at least twenty years ago. I picked up the cane and held it in front of me. The cane was more of a staff I supposed since it was taller than your average walking cane and a lot heavier. It was made from a dense wood and painted red and white to give it a holiday look. I smiled when I remembered the Christmas Gracie had first obtained the cane for the play. When the play was done, she let me play with it, and I remember using it as a magic portal to the North Pole and Santa's Village. At least it served as transport in my mind. I really had had an active imagination as a child. I guess that came from spending so much time alone up here in the attic.

I took the cane with me as I called to the cat and headed toward the door. I supposed I'd try to get a few hours of sleep before the sun came up. I wanted to head over to the library and speak to Hope first thing. I supposed I'd bring the cane along. We might be able to use it as a prop in Santa's House.

# Chapter 25

My late-night chat with Alastair had been helpful. I knew he was right in his assertion that if I had a question for Hope, I owed it to her to ask instead of harboring unconfirmed suspicions. I wanted to catch Hope before she got busy, so I decided to go to the library before I had breakfast. The library didn't open until nine, but I knew Hope was usually there by seven-thirty to shelve books and get the place ready to open. Hope was the library's only paid employee. Everyone else who staffed the place was a volunteer, so Hope made sure that she did everything she could to justify her salary.

When I arrived, the front door was open, which should have alerted me that something was up but didn't.

"Hope," I called out. "It's Callie. Are you here?"

I didn't see or hear anyone, but Hope's car had been in the lot, and the door had been open, so she had to be here somewhere.

"Hope," I called again. "I found a candy cane walking cane that I think will make an awesome prop for the Santa House. Are you here?"

I noticed the door to the room which held the reference books was open, so I headed in that direction. When I entered the room, I saw Hope tied to a chair with a piece of duct tape over her mouth. I started forward, but something in her eyes alerted me that I should actually drop and roll, which I did before I'd even had the chance to think it through. After I ended up on the floor on my back, I sat up and turned quickly, only to find a short and chubby man with a bat standing over me.

"Who are you?" the man demanded.

"A friend of the library here to do my volunteer shift." I held out a hand as if the gesture alone would somehow ward the man off.

"You're early," the man replied.

"I am. I like to arrive early to help get things ready for the day. Sometimes it's tough in the winter, it's just that... duck," I shouted after feigning a shocked expression and crossing my arms over my head.

The man must have responded to the panic in my voice since he lowered his head and crossed his arms over his head as if to protect himself from whatever was about to fall on him. This gave me a split second to jump up and scoot behind one of the floor-to-ceiling bookshelves.

"Very clever," the man said once he realized that something falling on his head had never been a possibility. "I won't fall for that again. Now, come on out."

I could see the man or at least portions of the man between the books that were lined on both sides of the stack. I slowly made my way around to the end of one of the rows. I circled around to the next row and waited. I could hear the man breathing, and occasionally, I could hear the scuffle of his boots. I knew if I was going to get out of this alive, I needed to keep my wits, so I continued to move slowly through the maze created by the rows and rows of bookshelves. Once I'd made my way to the end, I knew I'd need to double back. I needed to figure out a way to both escape and help Hope without getting either of us killed.

I tried to still my breathing so that the man with the bat wouldn't hear me and hone in on my location. Of course, all I really wanted to do was hyperventilate, so keeping my breath shallow and quiet was a challenge. Eventually, I was in the position I wanted. I could sense the man several rows over. The bookshelves were stacked back to back, so I knew that if I pushed on the books on my side of the stack, they would fall to the floor on the other side of the stack. Preparing to make my move, I set my body and then used my cane to push the books from the far side of the row onto the floor. The man came running toward the sound of the falling books. I only had a second to respond, but I managed to keep my wits as I looped my way around from the row where I'd been hiding, which allowed me to sneak up behind him. I raised my cane and hit the man as hard as I could while he was standing with his back to me. It didn't knock him out as I'd hoped, but it did divert his attention long enough for me to shove a book cart into his legs. That had him on his knees. I grabbed my cane and hit him again. It seemed to do the trick, and he fell helplessly to the floor.

"Are you okay?" I ran over to Hope.

"Tie him up. Hurry, he won't be out long."

I untied the ropes that had been secured around Hope's hands and feet, and then used them to tie up the man who I was sure had planned to kill both of us. As soon as he was secure, I called Cass, who promised to be right over.

"What happened?" I asked Hope after I allowed myself a moment to breathe.

"He was waiting for me when I arrived. He jumped me before I even knew he was there."

"Why?"

"For some reason, he thought I had Buford's money. He was determined to get it, and I was sure he was never going to let me go until he did. I'm sure he is the one who killed Buford and Ford. When he tied me up, he made a comment about not making the same mistake again. He said he was going to be sure to get the money before he let his temper get the best of him."

"Cass and I discussed the fact that Buford and Ford might have been killed by someone looking for Buford's money." I looked at the man, who I suspected would turn out to be Jason, the sister's kid. "I'm not sure if you heard, but part of the money was found in Ford's wall."

"I heard. Actually, I'm the one who told Cass to look for it in Ford's house."

I turned and looked Hope in the eye. "Are you Secret Santa?"

Hope froze. "Why would you ask that?"

"It has been theorized that Buford decided that he didn't want the money gifted to him by his sister. He didn't want the nephew to have it either, so he decided to give it away. Since he had no idea how to go about doing that, he enlisted the help of someone in the community with the resources and knowhow to determine who needed a gift from Secret Santa the most and how to get it to them. I thought about the people I'd interviewed and realized that when all was said and done, everyone who received a gift was linked to you in one way or another. It really does make perfect sense."

She shifted nervously in her seat. "You know that I can't confirm this suspicion of yours."

"Why not? What is so awful about being Secret Santa? Why don't you want anyone to know?"

Hope took my hand in hers. She gave it a squeeze and looked me in the eye. "Being Secret Santa isn't awful. It is a tremendous gift. A gift that has not only enriched my life but has enchanted the entire community as well. Revealing the identity of Secret Santa would strip away the wonder that everyone seems to feel. If you really think about it, the best part of the gift is the magic of not knowing, of letting the imagination you thought you'd lost somewhere along the way, run wild with possibility."

I knew Hope was right. I knew that by revealing Secret Santa's identity, I would be robbing the community of the fantasy that had captured everyone's imagination. I also knew that I had a responsibility to Dex. What I didn't know was what in the heck I was going to do.

# Chapter 26

## Friday

I'd given the situation a lot of thought and had finally come to a decision. My article wasn't due until Monday, but I had all the information I needed to wrap up the series, so I decided to turn it in early in order to give Dex the time he needed to do what he felt he needed to do. Hope hadn't been wrong when she'd said that the real magic of Secret Santa was embodied in his anonymity. It was the mystery and the magic of the whole thing that had brought the joy of the season to the small town of Foxtail Lake at a time when a lot of folks were having a hard time making their miracle happen. I really wanted a full-time job with the newspaper, but there was no way I was going to be the one to destroy everyone's fun.

Dex read the article as I sat watching. I could sense the myriad of emotions he might be feeling as a series of expressions crossed his face.

"So you couldn't figure out who Secret Santa was."

"I know who Secret Santa is. I'm choosing to keep that secret."

His lips tightened. "I see."

"I know I promised to reveal the name of the man or woman who has been running around town gifting those most in need with exactly what they need, but during the course of this journey, I've come to realize that there are more important things than having all the facts. There are mystery and magic and the ability to suspend disbelief just for a moment so that the lingering possibilities have a chance to be heard. There is the sheer joy that can be found in allowing the part of yourself that you thought had died in childhood out long enough to embrace the wonder that comes from not knowing who is behind the beard. I really, really love working here at the newspaper with you, and I really want to make a place for myself in the Foxtail News family, but I need to follow my heart, and my heart is telling me that it would be a mistake to rob the community of the fun they've been having."

He glanced down at the article in his hands. "I don't disagree. I've been feeling a little bad about the promise I made to my buddy at the Post. I'm sure he is not going to be happy that we aren't going to provide him with the expose he was hoping for."

"He still has a series to run, and I did turn in the story about Buford's inheritance and his death, as well as Ford's death by the same man. I suppose the Post has covered stories one would consider to be a bit more sensational, but the facts relating to the money Buford was gifted by his sister are pretty interesting."

Dex nodded. "The fact that the money was stolen was a bit of a shocker. Who would have guessed."

Certainly not me. When Cass had finally cornered Jason and compelled him to talk, Jason had shared the family secret that everyone related to Cornwall Norris had been keeping for more than sixty years. It seemed that Cornwall was a gangster of sorts back in the nineteen-thirties and forties. Before disappearing from his life in Chicago, he'd participated in almost a dozen bank robberies in seven states. At some point, Cornwall decided to get out while the getting was good, so he took his cut of the loot and moved to a small town just outside Denver. He met and married a woman named Rosa Walker, and together they had two children Hilde and Buford. Rosa died when her children were teenagers, and Cornwall moved the children to Salt Lake City. Eventually, Hilde married and moved to Denver, where she gave birth to a single child, Jason. When Cornwall died, he left what was left of the stolen money equally to Hilde and Buford, but neither child wanted to be associated with his ill-gotten gains, so they argued over what to do with it. Buford's way of dealing with the unpleasantness of his father's past was simply to ignore it, so he cut ties with his sister and moved up the mountain to Foxtail Lake.

Jason knew about the money and assumed that one day it would be his, so when his mother passed, and he found that Hilde had transferred the money to Buford before she died, Jason went a little crazy.

Buford and Hilde had considered the money a burden, and neither had ever wanted it, but it seemed that Jason wanted it very much. I suppose Buford had his reasons for not wanting Jason to have the money since as soon as he found out what his sister had done, he pulled the money out of the account Hilde had transferred it into and locked it in a drawer in his home. After Hilde died, he decided to dispose of the money once and for all. His father had obtained the money illegally, but Buford figured that if he gave the money away to those who needed it most, maybe the black stain that seemed to have been permanently attached to his family would somehow be lifted. He wasn't sure about how to go about distributing the money, so he went to Hope, who agreed to help him. When Buford found out that Jason was after the money, he asked his good friend, Ford, to hide it for him until Hope could dispose of all of it, which is how Ford became involved in the whole thing.

I, of course, wrote up the article to include the fact that both Buford and Ford had been killed over money that Buford's grandfather had stolen, but I left out Secret Santa and Hope's role in the whole thing. I decided that would not be a piece of the puzzle that would be revealed by me. I assumed that once the news of Buford's inheritance was made public, some people might suspect his role as Secret Santa, but suspecting wasn't knowing, so at least for a time, the magic would be left alive.

"The story is a good one, and I think the romance of an old-time gangster carrying out bank heists will appeal to the masses," Dex admitted. "I'll call my buddy and see what he wants to do. I wish I could have given him what he wanted, but maybe it is best this way. I really think the mystery of Secret Santa is going to be what draws in the reader and not the promise of a big reveal anyway. I just hope my friend from the Post feels the same way."

"So, you aren't going to fire me?"

He shook his head. "I would be stupid to do so. For one thing, you are an excellent journalist, who seems to know how to get right to the heart of things; and for another thing, with Brock gone, I really need you. In fact, I have two assignments I need to be done by the end of the day. You interested?"

"Absolutely. And thanks. I'll try not to let you down again."

He smiled. "You didn't let me down. I'm as caught up in the magic as everyone else. I'm not sure I want to know who is behind the gifts."

I exhaled slowly. "Thank you again. I'm really, really happy to be part of the Foxtail News family."

# Chapter 27

## Christmas Eve

"It looks like they are having fun," I said to Alastair as we watched Cass and Paisley ice skating on the lake from the attic window.

"Meow."

"Yes, I know that you are unhappy that Milo is spending the day with us, but he is a good dog who hasn't bothered you a bit. I suggest you make friends with him. Cass and I are spending more time together lately, and Milo comes as part of the package."

I hugged the cat to my chest, scratching him behind his ears as I watched the dog, the child, and the man I felt myself drawn to. I knew I was going to need to deal with the feelings I was developing for him at some point, but it was Christmas Eve, and today I just wanted to enjoy the fact that Gracie and Ethel were in the kitchen cooking up a storm, while Tom tinkered with the lights in the yard, and Alastair and I wrapped presents in the attic. I'd meant to have my gifts wrapped before this point, but Dex had been keeping me busy ever since I'd agreed to help him.

"I guess we should get back to the gift wrapping," I said to the cat. "Once we're done, we can go and join Cass and Paisley."

With that, the cat wiggled down and headed out the door. I supposed he wasn't thrilled with the idea of venturing out into the frosty day, but there was something about frostbite and Christmas that seemed to go together.

I glanced at my laptop and the article I'd been working on for the New Year's edition. I was far from being done, but at least I had started. I just hoped that the feature I'd been assigned for the following week would be less intense than the Secret Santa series. At least Dex seemed happy with the series, and his buddy, while disappointed there was no big reveal, went ahead and ran both my Christmas Eve story and the story about Cornwall Norris and the stash of money he left behind. Even in death, Cornwall had left behind a legacy of death and destruction. I felt bad for Buford, who'd simply been trying to do the right thing.

"Callie, are you up there in the attic?" Aunt Gracie called.

I headed to the top of the stairs and called back. "Yeah, I'm up here."

"Have you seen that big platter we use to serve the turkey? I can't find it anywhere."

"Hang on. I'll come down and look for it."

I turned and looked at the pile of gifts I'd wrapped. I still had a few to get to, but they could wait. I picked up the gifts that had been wrapped and headed toward the stairs. After placing the gifts beneath the tree, I headed into the pantry to look for the platter. I was sure I'd seen it buried beneath some other items when I was looking for the last jar of homemade jam.

"I got it," I said to Gracie as I slipped it out from under the dishes on top of it.

"Great. I thought I'd left it somewhere. Dinner will be in an hour if you want to let Cass and Paisley know they should start wrapping it up."

I pulled on my heavy coat, which had been left hanging on the rack. "Okay. I'll let them know. Tom, as well."

I headed out the door into the cold and snowy landscape. I headed toward Tom, who seemed to be doing more standing around than anything. "The lights look good."

"I know. I just like to tinker. I was about to head in and see if Gracie needs any help."

"She said dinner will be in an hour." I stood back and took in the house, the lights, and the movement that could be seen through the kitchen window. God, I'd missed this. The feeling of family. The feeling of belonging. During all those Christmases I'd chosen not to come home, I hadn't been aware of what I'd been missing out on, but now that I remembered how it felt to be home, I vowed never to miss another

Christmas with the people I loved the most in the world.

"Guess I should get inside," Tom said. "I like the hat."

I reached up to find the Santa hat I'd slipped on while wrapping gifts. I'd forgotten it was still there. "Seemed festive."

Tom leaned forward and kissed me on the cheek. "It is. And the sprig of mistletoe pinned to the brim is a nice touch."

I watched Tom as he walked away. I supposed I should remove the mistletoe before I came into contact with Cass. Reaching up, I unpinned it and put it into my jacket pocket.

"Are you coming out to skate?" Paisley, who had taken off her skates and slipped on her boots, ran over to me.

"Actually, I'm coming to tell you that dinner will be in an hour, so you should start to wrap it up. I'm sorry I wasn't able to join you, but I will tomorrow for sure."

"Okay. I'm cold anyway. I'm going to see if I can have some hot cocoa."

With that, she ran toward the house with Milo hot on her heels. I waited as Cass approached. "It looks like you were having fun."

He smiled. "The best time. Paisley is a good skater."

"She is," I nodded. "I'm supposed to let you know that dinner will be in an hour."

"Good. I'm starving." Cass took my hand and pulled me toward the lake. "I want to show you something."

I let myself be drug along behind him. He'd carved CC and CW intertwined in the ice.

"Remember when we did this when we were kids? Carved our initials in the ice," he asked.

"I do remember." My CC was on the top, and the C in Cass's name hung from the second C in my name and was followed by a very flowery W. "I'd forgotten all about that."

"We vowed to be best friends forever. We promised to skate on this lake every winter and to carve our initials in the ice."

"We did," I acknowledged.

"It seems," Cass said, turning so we were facing each other, "that we have some time to make up for."

I lowered my eyes. "I know. I'm sorry. It was my fault we didn't keep that promise. I left, but you were here waiting."

He ran a finger along my jaw, pausing at my chin to tilt my head up. "I understand why you left. You've always been one to follow your heart, and your heart led you elsewhere. I'm not happy that you lost your career, but I am happy you're back."

"I know. Me too."

He reached into my pocket and took out the mistletoe I thought I'd cleverly hidden. He held it over our heads.

"I don't think…" I started.

He leaned forward and softly touched his lips to mine before I could complete my protest. I wanted to pull back, but instead, I found my arms around his neck.

"Merry Christmas, Calliope Rose," he whispered against my lips.

"Merry Christmas to you as well, Deputy Wylander."

# Next From Kathi Daley Books

# Preview

At what point does a concerned bystander become a stalker?

I'd been asking myself that a lot lately. I'd first met Star Moonwalker six weeks ago, when I'd stopped by her antique store during my route as a US Postal Service carrier to deliver a certified letter. After a brief discussion, in which the woman revealed to me that she'd first moved to White Eagle to search for her birth parents, I'd discovered that she was most likely my half sister. I'd also discovered that the man she'd hired to track down her biological parents, a private investigator named Sam Denton, very well might have been killed by a man I suspected could be my own father.

Of course, my father being the killer was not the only explanation. It was also possible that Sam Denton had been killed by the same people who were after my father, forcing him to fake his own death fifteen years ago. Either way, I suspected that Star might be in danger because she had continued to dig around in my father's past even after Denton's death, so I'd been keeping an eye on her, hence the stalking.

Not that Star had been aware that I'd been watching her or digging into her past. I'd been very covert in my approach. I'd started by having my boyfriend, Tony Marconi, do a very quiet computer search into her history, while I began spending time in the woman's antique store, trying to get to know her better. I still didn't know everything I needed to about the events that occurred at the time of Star's birth, so I'd been unable to conclusively determine that she and I shared the same biological father, but it did appear as if my father had been traveling with Star's mother at the time immediately preceding her birth.

"Tess Thomas?" the woman on the other end of the phone line asked.

"Yes, this is Tess." I'd been sitting in my car on hold for a good fifteen minutes, waiting to hear the results of the DNA tests I'd mailed away several weeks before.

"The two samples that you sent do not indicate a familial link."

I narrowed my eyes. "So the individuals who supplied the two samples are not related?"

"The genetic profiles of the individuals providing the samples demonstrate that it is statistically unlikely a blood relationship exists. A detailed report will be sent to the address you provided within a week. Is there anything else I can help you with?"

"No. Thank you." I hung up and then turned and looked at my dog, Tilly, who'd been waiting patiently with me. "Well, what do you know about that?"

Tilly shoved her nose into my lap. I looked back toward the house where I'd discovered Star lived. I'd been so certain that she was my half sister that I'd actually dug through her garbage to retrieve a piece of chewing gum I'd seen her throw away to gain a sample of her DNA that I could have compared to my own. At that time I'd thought the DNA test would simply serve as a confirmation of what I was sure I already knew. How could I have been so wrong?

I focused on the colorful Christmas lights Star had hung along the eaves and around the door and windows as the interior light in a downstairs room went off. A half minute later, a light in one of the upstairs rooms went on. I'd decided the room on the second story at the front of the house must be some sort of workroom or office. Star spent a lot of time in that room when she was home. I slowly stroked Tilly's head as I watched a shadow move across the room. I supposed I really should go before someone noticed me sitting out here. I'd been so sure that Star was my half sister that I'd never even stopped to consider an alternate explanation as to what had occurred when she'd been abandoned by a man I was sure was my father.

I pulled my seat belt across my chest but hesitated to start the engine. The snow that had been threatening all day had begun to fall. I knew I should head home, yet I hesitated. I certainly didn't know everything there was to know about Star's past, but what I did had seemed to support my sister theory. Three years ago, after her adoptive parents passed away, Star had hired Denton to find her birth parents. Through his research, the private investigator found evidence that suggested that Star had been surrendered to a church when she was just hours old. He'd followed up on this evidence and was able to confirm that a man had left the baby with a nun after informing her that the baby's mother had died and she needed a home. The nun had tried to get additional information about the baby and her parents from the man, but he'd refused to answer any questions. Once the baby was safely in the nun's arms, he left. Star had been adopted by wonderful parents and hadn't looked back until after they died.

During his investigation, Denton found out that on the same day Star had been dropped off at the church in Great Falls, Montana, a woman was found shot to death in Buffalo, Wyoming. It was noted in the police report filed after her death that the victim had recently given birth. The detective in charge of the murder case looked for the baby in Wyoming, but the infant was never found. For reasons unknown to me, the investigator did not look for the baby outside that state, so the link to Star was never discovered.

That is, until Denton came along and put two and two together. After Star realized that the woman who was shot was most likely her biological mother, and that her mother had met with a violent end, she'd decided to give up the idea of searching for answers about her past. She'd paid off the PI and asked him not to look for her father.

A couple of years later, the same PI was asked by a totally different client to find proof that a man who had been living under an alias for years and who everyone believed to be dead, was actually still alive. During the course of his backtracking to figure out what had really happened to that guy, Denton came across the report filed by the detective who'd been assigned to investigate the murder of the woman who'd been shot in Buffalo just prior to Star being left at the church in Great Falls. Denton realized immediately that the woman mentioned in the report was the same one he believed was Star's mother, and that was when it occurred to me that the man Denton had been hired to find was could be my father.

That was confirmed in my mind when Star told me that the owner of the apartment building her biological mother had been staying in when she was shot had identified the man traveling with her was the same man who had dropped off the baby at the church. Star had a copy of the driver's license of that man, and the photo on it was that of a young Grant Thomas, my father, though the name on it was Grant Tucker, a name Tony and I already suspected he'd used as an alias at one point in his life.

"So Grant Tucker, aka Grant Thomas, was traveling with Star's biological mother but was not her biological father? Why?" I asked Tilly.

She licked my cheek in reply.

I looked down when my phone dinged, indicating I had a text. It was from Tony, wondering what time I'd be home for dinner. I texted back, letting him know I'd had a stop to make but would be home shortly. Once that was accomplished, I turned my attention back to Tilly.

"I suppose it is possible that Star's mother was in some sort of trouble and was on the run from whoever eventually shot her." I let that idea roll around in my mind a bit. "I also suppose that Dad could have been with her to help her escape. Maybe he was a friend of Star's biological mother, or maybe he was some sort of bodyguard." I'd suspected for a while that my dad might work, or at least have worked in the past, for some sort of government agency, such as the CIA.

I hated to think that my father had killed Denton, but he had gone to a lot of trouble to disappear fifteen years ago and the PI had done a heck of a good job tracking him down. Denton had even managed to provide recent photos of my dad for the man who'd hired him. I knew my dad would not have taken kindly to that.

When Tony and I had tried to track Dad down, we'd met with a ton of resistance, culminating in his rare appearance to tell me to back off. As I thought back on that encounter, I had to admit that he'd seemed more scared than angry. He'd told me that not only had my search put him in danger, but it also put Mom, my brother Mike, and me in danger as well. I still had no idea why Dad needed to appear to be dead, but I'd been researching him for long enough to know that the people around him tended to die, so maybe he'd been justified in his concern.

Tilly put a paw on my lap and I looked into her big brown eyes. It was late and the snow was getting harder. I knew we should head home before Tony began to worry about us. I put my hand on the ignition as a dark blue sedan pulled into Star's driveway. A tall man, dressed casually in a black leather jacket and denim pants, got out and headed to the front door. I realized that Star might have a date. I didn't recognize the guy, but I also couldn't really see his face; the sun set early at this time of the year, so even though it was only around six o'clock, it was already pitch dark. I decided to wait to start my vehicle because I didn't want to draw attention to myself. I figured the man would either go inside or Star would come out and they'd both leave together. I watched as the front porch light went on. Star opened the door, said something, and then fell to the ground. Immediately afterward, the man returned to his car and drove off.

"Did that man just shoot Star?" I asked Tilly. I opened my car door just as the vehicle that had been parked in Star's drive pulled away. I ran across the street toward the still-open front door. Star lay lifeless across the threshold. "Oh God." I pulled out my cell and called Mike, who was a cop. "There's been a shooting," I informed him. "It's Star Moonwalker." I provided the address and told him to hurry.

Mike instructed me to stay put, so I did. I could see that Star was dead, but I felt for a pulse just to be sure, then I called Tilly and walked away from the body. I didn't want to leave Star alone, but I knew better than to do anything to contaminate the crime scene, so I walked toward the far end of the porch and sat down.

In that moment, I wasn't sure what to do. What to feel. On one hand, until minutes before she'd been shot, I'd believed Star to be my half sister, which had created a false sense of connection between us. On the other hand, I'd only met her about six weeks earlier and didn't know her all that well. I supposed once the shock wore off I'd be able to sort out my mixed emotions. Right now, profound grief was all tied up with fear, disbelief, and most of all anger. Someone had killed an innocent woman whose seemingly only crime had been curiosity about her birth parents. Star had been a nice woman with a natural presence, a calm manner, and a casual style, reminiscent of the flower children of the 1960s. There certainly didn't seem as if anything could be gained by killing her, and yet someone had.

Despite the fact that I'd been too far away to get a good look at the man who'd pulled up, rung the doorbell, and killed Star, I was pretty sure it had not been my father. This man was tall, as was my father, but my dad had broad shoulders and this man had appeared to be so thin as to be described as wiry. Of course, the fact that my father had most likely not been the gunman himself didn't mean this man hadn't been hired to do it by the man I'd once called dad.

I let my mind drift to the man I now think of as a ghost. Grant Thomas was officially deceased, so while that meant he no longer lived, he wasn't really dead either. Prior to Tony uncovering a photo of my father taken three years after his supposed death, I honestly believed that he'd been killed in a truck accident when I was fourteen. I'm not sure why my mind hadn't accepted the fact that my father was dead, but there had always been a part of me that fantasized that the man who was burned so badly as to be unidentifiable was not actually the same man I knew as my father. Tony, being the genius he was even back then, agreed to dig around. It had taken him twelve years to find the photo, but once he had proof of life after the accident, I'd grabbed onto the mystery and hadn't let go of it ever since. Of course, the more I dug, the more I learned and the more disturbed I became.

I watched as Mike pulled up along the street in front of the house. He headed up the front steps, knelt down in front of the body to check for a pulse, and then looked in my direction. "Are you okay?"

I nodded.

"What happened?"

I hesitated. I couldn't very well tell my brother that I'd been watching this woman from across the street without going into a lot more explanation than I was willing to at this point, so I told him that I'd been driving by, heard a gunshot, saw a blue sedan pull away from the house, and had gone to check it out, which is when I saw the woman stretched out dead across the threshold.

"Did you know this woman?" Mike asked.

"Sort of. As I said, her name is Star Moonwalker. She owns an antique store in town. I deliver mail to her sometimes, and when I have time I stop in and look around while I am there. We chat while I look, so in a way you could say we knew each other."

Mike took out his handheld radio and spoke to Frank Hudson, his second in command. He confirmed that the coroner was on the way, and then he returned his attention to me. "I need to process the scene and see to the removal of the body. I am going to want to ask you some additional questions then. If you'd like, I can come by your cabin to talk to you when I'm done here."

I nodded. "Okay. That sounds good. It is getting pretty cold."

"Can you describe the person who drove away from the scene?"

"Male. Tall. Black leather jacket, denim pants. It was dark, so I didn't see his face."

"And the car?"

"A blue sedan. A Ford, I think, but I'm not sure. I do know it was one of those midsize sedans. I didn't notice the license plate, I'm afraid. The whole thing happened so fast that it seems it was over before I knew to pay attention."

"And you were just driving by?" Mike asked.

I glanced at the ground and nodded. I could see that Mike didn't believe me, and I knew he wasn't going to let this go, but Frank pulled up just then, so Mike walked Tilly and me back across the street to my Jeep. He opened the door and Tilly jumped up. I slid in after her.

"I'll be by when I can. In the meantime, I want you to write down everything you can remember," Mike instructed through the open driver's side window as I adjusted my seat belt.

"Okay."

"And Tess—"

I took a chance and looked him in the eye. "Yeah?"

"When I come by, I'm going to want the rest of the story."

I swallowed and nodded. He kissed me on the cheek, then stepped away. He closed the door, and I started the ignition and pulled away.

Mike knew that Dad was still alive. I'd finally broken down and told him a year ago. But he didn't know the rest. The part I'd been keeping from him. I wasn't exactly sure how he'd react, but I knew him well enough to be sure he wasn't going to be happy about any of it. I supposed I knew that one day I'd have to confess everything; I just hadn't realized when I'd left work for the weekend that that day was today.

As I drove toward the cabin where Tony, his dog Titan, and my cats Tang and Tinder were waiting, I felt my stress level increase dramatically. I supposed it might be the result of delayed reaction from the shooting, but I supposed it could also have been heightened by my impending conversation with Mike. I knew it was going to be unpleasant. The truth of the matter was that I'd known our dad was alive a full year before I'd even brought Mike in on the secret. Mike was a good guy and I trusted him implicitly, but he was also pretty intense. He tended to act before thinking when it came to protecting the people he loved, so I rightfully feared he'd only make things worse if he knew our father was still alive and kicking in the world.

Of course, even after I'd shared with Mike the proof Tony and I had found of the existence of the man we both thought had died years before, I hadn't continued to fill him in on every little detail of our investigation, as I'd promised I would. I hadn't told him that Dad had shown up at the hospital when Mike was shot and had almost died, and I hadn't told him about Star or the suspicion I'd had that she was our half sister. Though my suspicion had turned out to be wrong, our dad had been involved with her mother in some way. I was sure he'd been the one to drop her off at the church, so whether he was her father or not, he'd been connected to her from the beginning.

Deep in my heart, I was sure that it was this connection that had led to her death. Maybe I should have done more to warn her that digging around in the past of Grant Thomas, or Grant Tucker as it might be, could only lead to trouble for everyone involved. Maybe instead of watching her from afar, I should have confronted her about the envelope I'd delivered to her when we first met. An envelope she'd told me contained a copy of the file Sam Denton had built on the man I was certain was my father. Denton must have known his life was in danger, because he'd given a copy of his file to a friend for safekeeping. The friend knew about Star's situation and had decided to send it to her after Denton's death.

I turned onto the narrow road leading out to my cabin. The file had concerned me from the beginning, but Star had assured me that she'd locked it away in her safety deposit box. She'd told me she hadn't read it after she'd opened it in my presence on the day I delivered it, and had no idea what was in it. I didn't know what sort of evidence Denton had managed to dig up, but apparently, it was damaging enough to cause someone to decide to end the life of both the PI who'd built the file and the woman who'd currently been in possession of it.

# Books by Kathi Daley
Come for the murder, stay for the romance

## The Inn at Holiday Bay:
Boxes in the Basement
Letters in the Library
Message in the Mantel
Answers in the Attic
Haunting in the Hallway
Pilgrim in the Parlor
Note in the Nutcracker – *December 2019*

## A Cat in the Attic Mystery:
The Curse of Hollister House
The Mystery Before Christmas
The Secret of Logan Pond – *January 2020*

## Zoe Donovan Cozy Mystery:
Halloween Hijinks
The Trouble With Turkeys
Christmas Crazy
Cupid's Curse
Big Bunny Bump-off
Beach Blanket Barbie
Maui Madness
Derby Divas
Haunted Hamlet
Turkeys, Tuxes, and Tabbies

Christmas Cozy
Alaskan Alliance
Matrimony Meltdown
Soul Surrender
Heavenly Honeymoon
Hopscotch Homicide
Ghostly Graveyard
Santa Sleuth
Shamrock Shenanigans
Kitten Kaboodle
Costume Catastrophe
Candy Cane Caper
Holiday Hangover
Easter Escapade
Camp Carter
Trick or Treason
Reindeer Roundup
Hippity Hoppity Homicide
Firework Fiasco
Henderson House
Holiday Hostage
Lunacy Lake
Celtic Christmas – *December 2019*

Zimmerman Academy The New Normal
Zimmerman Academy New Beginnings
Ashton Falls Cozy Cookbook

# Whales and Tails Cozy Mystery:
Romeow and Juliet
The Mad Catter
Grimm's Furry Tail
Much Ado About Felines
Legend of Tabby Hollow

Cat of Christmas Past
A Tale of Two Tabbies
The Great Catsby
Count Catula
The Cat of Christmas Present
A Winter's Tail
The Taming of the Tabby
Frankencat
The Cat of Christmas Future
Farewell to Felines
A Whisker in Time
The Catsgiving Feast
A Whale of a Tail
The Catnap Before Christmas
A Mew Beginning – *March 2020*

# A Tess and Tilly Mystery:
The Christmas Letter
The Valentine Mystery
The Mother's Day Mishap
The Halloween House
The Thanksgiving Trip
The Saint Paddy's Promise
The Halloween Haunting
The Christmas Clause
The Firework Folly – *June 2020*

# Rescue Alaska Mystery:
Finding Justice
Finding Answers
Finding Courage
Finding Christmas
Finding Shelter – *January 2020*

# The Hathaway Sisters:
Harper
Harlow
Hayden – *February 2020*

# Writers' Retreat Mystery:
First Case
Second Look
Third Strike
Fourth Victim
Fifth Night
Sixth Cabin
Seventh Chapter
Eighth Witness
Ninth Grave

# Haunting by the Sea:
Homecoming by the Sea
Secrets by the Sea
Missing by the Sea
Betrayal by the Sea
Thanksgiving by the Sea
Christmas by the Sea

# Tj Jensen Paradise Lake Mystery:
Pumpkins in Paradise
Snowmen in Paradise
Bikinis in Paradise
Christmas in Paradise
Puppies in Paradise
Halloween in Paradise
Treasure in Paradise
Fireworks in Paradise

Beaches in Paradise
Thanksgiving in Paradise

# Sand and Sea Hawaiian Mystery:
Murder at Dolphin Bay
Murder at Sunrise Beach
Murder at the Witching Hour
Murder at Christmas
Murder at Turtle Cove
Murder at Water's Edge
Murder at Midnight
Murder at Pope Investigations

# Seacliff High Mystery:
The Secret
The Curse
The Relic
The Conspiracy
The Grudge
The Shadow
The Haunting

# Road to Christmas Romance:
Road to Christmas Past

*USA Today* best-selling author Kathi Daley lives in beautiful Lake Tahoe with her husband Ken. When she isn't writing, she likes spending time hiking the miles of desolate trails surrounding her home. She has authored more than a hundred books in twelve series. Find out more about her books at www.kathidaley.com

Stay up-to-date:
Newsletter, *The Daley Weekly* http://eepurl.com/NRPDf
Webpage – www.kathidaley.com
Facebook at Kathi Daley Books – www.facebook.com/kathidaleybooks
Kathi Daley Books Group Page – https://www.facebook.com/groups/569578823146850/
E-mail – kathidaley@kathidaley.com
Twitter at Kathi Daley@kathidaley – https://twitter.com/kathidaley
Amazon Author Page – https://www.amazon.com/author/kathidaley
BookBub – https://www.bookbub.com/authors/kathi-daley

Cameron Park

Made in the
USA
Middletown, DE